The Midsummer Treasures

A HARRY FOX ORIGIN STORY

ANDREW CLAWSON

Golden Idol Publishing

Contents

Chapter 1

County Kilkenny, Ireland

A crow nearly took his head off.

Cawing erupted as Harry Fox ducked, his foot slipping on the slick limestone cave floor and nearly sending him sprawling. He could only shake his head. *The gods are watching.*

He checked the notebook in his hands. The scrawled words he'd jotted down shook for a moment. "It's just a bird," he said to himself. "The gods have better things to worry about than you."

Dripping water echoed as he walked on. *Eighty-six. Eighty-seven.* Every step clocked in his head on a silent counter. Exactly as the instructions stated. One more step and he finally moved out of the long patch of sunlight that had stretched from the cave mouth into the tunnel, cooler air wrapping him in an unwelcome embrace as he pushed ahead and forced everything from his mind but the steps. Only nine hundred more to go. If you believed a random set of instructions cut into a hunk of stone two thousand years ago, that is.

The hairs on his arm rose as a rustling noise sounded from far ahead. Birds or snakes upset at an intruder? Perhaps ancient Celtic deities feeling the same? Harry's jaw tightened. *Doesn't matter. Wait until they see what I find. That'll show them.* He kept counting and walked ahead, following the beam of his headlamp as darkness pushed in on all sides and the soft whistle of a damp breeze reached his ears.

His fingers brushed across the hunk of stone tucked into a back pocket. About the size of a paperback novel, the stone had dense script cut into it. A story. Make-believe, if you asked anyone else. Anyone except Harry. The Latin words told a fantastical tale that had captured his eye. That's why Harry had demanded the tablet be part of the trade he'd made recently. A simple relic trade, Harry giving another relic hunter an Egyptian vase in exchange for a Roman statue. But this tablet had been among the other man's wares, and one glance at the Latin script had made Harry ask for it to be included in the trade. The man had agreed, and Harry now had a lead. A lead on a quest that couldn't possibly exist.

A quest tied to an ancient people who'd lived on these lands thousands of years ago and held fast against the most fearsome army of their time. A people whose ancestors still lived here, and who still carried the memories of their forefathers. The Irish of centuries ago, long before this land was called Ireland, had left a message tied to their gods, the Celtic deities based on nature worship that venerated the forces of nature and the natural world. Thousands of years ago at this time, they had celebrated the long days of mid-summer. Today, Harry was attempting to unravel their mystery.

The pungent smell of decay and wet earth filled his nose. Dunmore Cave was well known across Ireland and beyond. A small hoard of silver and bronze antiquities had been found here, though the cave was much more notorious for the Viking massacre that had taken place in it. One thousand men, women and children had been killed, native Irish murdered by marauding Vikings. Nobody knew the true story of why so many had died here. The tale laid out on the tablet Harry carried might solve the mystery.

No light penetrated this far into the cavern. Harry lightly touched the rough stone walls on either side to keep his bearings, the rock slick to his touch and barren of any markings. No drawings, no inscriptions. Nothing to show this ancient tunnel now held anything other than the promise of a broken leg and a chance to add one more set of bones to the Viking pile. One corner of his lip turned up.

"One thousand."

He stopped. He looked left, then right. Nothing but blank stone and patches of green moss looked back. Harry frowned. He pulled the tablet from his pocket and read the Latin inscription again.

Travel one thousand paces into Brigid's temple above River Dinan. Reach for the Morrigan. Have the courage of the Tuatha to proceed.

Brigid was a prominent goddess in pre-Christian Ireland, a member of a supernatural race called the *Tuatha Dé Danann* who were worshipped in this land so long ago. This cave had been a primary temple for her worship, and the only temple located on the River Dinan. Harry was certain this cave was the correct place. He'd walked one thousand steps into it, and found no *Morrigan* to reach for. *The Morrigan* was at times described as one god, but at other times as three, a trio of sisters.

The *Morrigan*, however many existed, was often depicted in Irish mythology as a crow. War and fate were tied to her, as she could allegedly predict death or victory in battle. Harry scratched the stubble on his chin as he searched. No crows to be found.

A drop of water landed on his forehead. He looked up. His gaze narrowed. "Look at that."

The carving was nearly invisible even with his headlamp shining on it. A bird had been cut into the cavern roof. A crow. His fingers tingled as he reached to touch it. And came up short. Harry Fox was of average height on a good day. No way could he reach the bird carved into the cave roof ten feet above him. "Nobody could reach that," he said.

A pile of fallen rocks to one side called for his attention. Several large rocks, nearly all of them roughly square-shaped. His gaze narrowed. These were too convenient. If this cavern wall had partially collapsed, the stones would be small and rougher, not shaped like—like *stepping stones*.

"These were left here on purpose."

Natural stones didn't fall so perfectly formed from a cave wall. These had been quarried, then roughened around the edges and laid here. He tugged at the topmost block and leapt aside as it toppled to the ground, rolling to a spot almost exactly beneath the carved crow.

Harry did not move to stand on it. He was too busy staring at a hole in the wall. A hole that had been hidden behind the stacked stones.

Harry leaned over and examined the hole. His chest tightened. An image had been carved inside the hole, that of a crow in flight. "Reach for the Morrigan," he said to himself. What had seemed like nonsense now made sense. An image on the cave ceiling to get his attention, and this carving in the hole in the wall to complete the message. Harry hesitated. Normally, the last thing he'd do with a hole in a cave wall was stick his arm inside. That sort of behavior tended to get you killed.

He angled his neck so the headlamp beam penetrated farther into the opening. A narrow stone hung down from the top of the hole perhaps two feet in. Hung down, but didn't touch the bottom of the shaft. It took him a second. "It's a handle."

Any thoughts of avoiding arm-crushing traps disappeared as he reached in, his arm going into the dark hole up to his shoulder until he could grasp the stone handle. Moisture and the chilled stone set his arm hair on edge. Cobwebs caught his fingers as he maneuvered for a better grip. Harry gritted his teeth, then pulled.

Rock scraped on rock deep within the wall as the handle moved toward him. It resisted, then, without warning, slid so that he had to take a step back until the handle held fast. He pulled once more to be certain, then whipped his arm out before anything in the hole decided to keep it. The noise of grinding stone echoed in the cave. He peered at the handle. It wasn't moving. The grating noise became so loud it buried any other noises, a thunder that filled his ears.

Dry air floated across his neck as the rumbling stopped. A second, much larger hole appeared across the cave. A large section of the wall had dropped to reveal a second tunnel running off the main one. The sound of grating stone finished echoing as he moved to the new opening. No visible drawings, crow or otherwise. Harry took one step into the cave and paused, breathing deeply. *Dad is gonna love this.*

Fred Fox had recovered, sold and otherwise handled more undiscovered ancient relics than Harry could count. He didn't think Harry's gut instinct that Dunmore Cave held a secret was true, but he'd also taught Harry to trust his gut. Harry took another step into the cave, checking for signs of danger, then headed in.

His headlamp pushed back the dark as he moved. Perhaps thirty feet in his light found the danger. Harry stopped.

A rope bridge lay in front of him. It was covered in black tar, the dark rope guiderails on either side attached to wood boards that formed a walkway. He knelt in front of the first plank and knocked on the board. Hard as a rock. The chasm below was deep enough that his headlamp beam didn't reach the bottom. Harry picked up a small rock and dropped it into the black pit. The rock fell for a long time before it hit bottom.

The bridge was maybe twenty feet across, long enough that no one short of an Olympic long jumper could make the leap. He directed his light beyond the bridge's far end to the cave's rear wall a short distance beyond. Several pedestals stood in front of the wall, with objects resting on them. He couldn't clearly see what they were. Not yet.

The first bridge plank held when he stepped on it. Harry gripped the tar-coated ropes and walked forward. The bridge protested and the ropes creaked, but the planks held. Another step, then another, until he was halfway across. He kept his eyes ahead, only glancing up when a shadow on the ceiling caught his attention.

"There's another handle."

A curved stone handle extended down from the ceiling to a point not far above his head. A small crow was carved into the handle. "Reach for the Morrigan." He grabbed the handle and pulled. It held fast; he shifted his weight as he tugged again, so hard that one foot went to the next board. That board collapsed. Harry shouted, grabbing the handle with two hands to keep his balance. His full body weight did the trick and the handle moved down as he nearly pitched forward. He stepped back onto a sturdy board as the loose one fell into the abyss.

Harry let go of the handle above him and grabbed the guide ropes on either side. A grinding noise sounded and he kept still as two parallel lengths of stone moved out from the far edge of the pit, sliding below the wooden boards until they stopped beneath his feet. He cautiously leaned over to look closely. Identical stone supports had been below his feet the entire time as he crossed the first half of the bridge. Now these new supports held the second half of the crossing.

Harry made it across the rest of the bridge without incident and stood on solid ground again. Three waist-high stone pillars stood in front of him. A small wooden model ship was on top of every pillar. Each galley-style ship included two masts and long oars protruding on either side. The stone wall behind the pillars had long cracks across it so that several sections of the stone looked ready to drop free if it weren't for the long vines snaking across the wall to hold those sections in place.

The only other object from the ancient Britons was a single torch hanging on the wall. A torch, three pillars and three replica ships.

A tar-like covering coated each ship, similar to the substance covering the bridge. Whoever had put all this here had wanted to preserve the wood. Surely the early Britons wouldn't have expected it to take this long for any message to be uncovered. If the tar coating wasn't meant to preserve for millennia, then what was its purpose? Harry's gaze went to the torch.

"That stuff looks flammable." A memory called to him. A story he'd read while researching the *Tuatha Dé Danann*. Legend said the mythological race traveled to Ireland in ships, and upon landing immediately burned their ships to show their commitment to remain in their new homeland. Harry looked at the torch again. "They put this here for a reason."

What if this was a test? The mythical beings believed so strongly in themselves that they had destroyed their way back home. Courageous? Or foolish? Perhaps both, but that sort of commitment impressed. Did Harry need to show the same faith now? Was this a test of his commitment to move ahead?

"It's worth a shot." He pulled the torch from its holder on the wall. Nothing. He took a lighter from his pocket and flame erupted when he flicked the wheel. The thick rushes of the torch burst to life, its deep orange light filling the cavern. Thick smoke sent ghostly shadows across the walls as the flame strengthened. Harry stepped toward one pillar, narrowed his eyes against the acrid smoke, and touched his torch to the wood ship.

The ship erupted in flame, the pitch coating it melting and popping as the vessel became an inferno. The flames burned bright for several beats, snatches of flame falling loose or shooting away until nothing remained of the ship but choking smoke. Harry waved away the fumes and found a stone fulcrum had been hidden beneath the wooden ship. As he watched, the length of stone resembling a playground seesaw flipped so that the end that had been beneath the wooden ship rose and the opposite end fell. Harry flinched. The cave failed to kill him.

The next two ships burned away to reveal two additional levers. Nothing happened when the second lever fell. The third lever flipped sides to no effect. Harry had enough time to wonder if he'd missed something before a dust cloud erupted from the rear wall and a panel opened in the wall behind the center pillar, revealing a chamber.

"Another tablet."

Harry reached toward the stone tablet sitting inside. A piece of burning vine fell, the last licks of flame from his ship-burning efforts. Shadows and shifting light from his torch obscured the Latin letters inscribed on it. He hesitated with his fingers brushing the tablet, steeled himself, and shifted the small tablet. Embers fell like tiny fireflies landing. He moved his torch so that the tablet face came into view.

Crack. Dust shot from a crevice in the chamber wall. Harry stepped back as a stone broke free from the rear wall and a burning vine snapped. More rocks broke free, dust filled the air and a spark from his torch hit a thick vine across the cracked rear wall. The vine burst into flame. A rock the size of his torso came loose and fell directly on top of the center pillar. The rock crashed down before he could push it aside, smashing the lever on the central pillar before bouncing to the right and pushing that lever down as well.

The ground shook, ancient mechanisms coming alive as the floor rumbled and he went down to one knee. Harry turned and his stomach dropped. He jumped to his feet and ran.

The bridge was collapsing behind him. The closest planks were dropping into the abyss. Every racing step he took saw two other planks falling away. Half the bridge had vanished. He couldn't make that leap. No way. His gaze narrowed on one object. Harry cradled the tablet like a football and accelerated toward it. *Don't miss.* He planted his foot at the edge of the void and jumped. Legs kicking, he dropped the torch and flew across the emptiness with one hand out. Harry didn't look down. He reached out.

And grabbed the Morrigan handle.

Got it. He latched onto the handle, pulling as his weight carried him forward. He kicked both feet ahead as his arm shouted and he hurled himself toward the far edge of the abyss. He cleared the edge with inches to spare. Feet first, Harry slid across the far floor and came to a stop. He twisted and looked down at the grave that wouldn't be his today. A large rock broke loose from the ceiling and nearly took his head off before he twisted and jumped up, racing toward the tunnel mouth as the ceiling collapsed around him. Dust filled the air and his brain rattled. A deafening noise almost knocked him down as the walls crumbled around him. Harry took one final step and dove for the light of the longer main tunnel.

He crashed into the main tunnel, sliding across the ground until he stopped as his head smacked into the far wall. He flipped over and looked behind him. The entrance to the side tunnel was gone. The retracting cover had moved back into place to hide any trace the secret cavern had ever existed.

Harry got unsteadily to his feet. The stone tablet remained tightly clenched under one arm. He wiped dirt from his face and couldn't help but grin as he jogged out of Dunmore Cave into the brilliant Irish sun.

The adventure had definitely begun.

Chapter 2

County Kilkenny, Ireland

"I found another tablet."

A car the size of a small side table puttered past as Harry sat outside a café in Kilkenny, holding his phone to his ear. Clusters of brilliant pink flowers hung from pots alongside streetlamp posts running the length of the street. Tourists and locals walked along the row of restaurants and small shops lining either side, few of them glancing at the bedraggled man at a table by himself underneath a cafe awning. The pint glass in front of him was nearly empty.

Fred Fox had seen much of the world. Very little surprised him. "You *what?*"

Harry did not hide his excitement. "I found another tablet, Dad. In the cave."

"Dunmore Cave has been explored inside and out," Fred said. "Where did you find it?"

Harry explained about following the Morrigan symbols to reveal the handle that led to an entirely new cave. Fred didn't interrupt as Harry detailed burning replica ships before the cave and bridge collapsed around him. When Harry stopped talking, his father offered a sound that could have been approval. Harry took a long drink from his beer. "What do you think?" Harry asked.

"Two things," Fred said. "One, you're lucky you didn't get yourself killed." Harry knew enough to keep quiet. "Two," Fred continued. "Well done."

A heat crept up Harry's torso from stomach to neck. "Thanks."

"Anything readable on the second tablet?"

Harry angled the stone to catch the sunlight. "More than writing. There are Latin words, and four images."

"Do you recognize the images?" Fred asked.

"It's the Four Treasures of the Tuatha Dé Danann."

"The supernatural race from Irish mythology."

"You only know that because I told you."

"Fortunately for you, I do not dismiss information solely based on the source."

Harry grumbled before responding. "The name means 'folk of the goddess Danu,' one of their gods. The Tuatha are variously described as kings, queens, warriors or heroes. They all have supernatural powers, yet interact with humans. What matters now is the legend of the Four Treasures they are said to have brought to Ireland."

"Where they burned their ships."

"You were paying attention," Harry said. "The treasures have magical properties. There's a stone that cries out when the rightful king stands on it, a spear that guarantees victory to anyone who wields it in battle, an irresistible sword you can't escape from if it's drawn against you, and a cauldron that makes everyone who gathers around it satisfied. The sword is the most powerful of the treasures and is a last resort, to be used if the other defenses fail. To draw it is to unleash the wrath of their goddess of death."

"Each treasure is inscribed on the tablet you found?" Harry confirmed it was true. "What words are on it?" Fred asked.

"A single line of text," Harry said. "Under the stone image. There's nothing below the other treasures. Side note, the only treasure most believe existed is the stone. It's called the Fal Stone, and it's standing not far from where I am now."

"That could be relevant," Fred said.

"Wait until you hear this." Harry first read the text in Latin, then translated to English. "*The four sides of Danu's cross show the way as she touches the world.*"

Fred repeated the statement back to Harry before posing a question. "Any thoughts on what it means?"

Harry had given this due consideration before calling Fred. This was Harry's first solo relic hunt. Fred Fox could finish a quest like this in his sleep. Harry now had a chance to move out of his father's shadow. "I think the sentence being below the stone is significant," Harry said. "It's the only treasure whose location I know."

"How long has the stone been where it is now?"

"Since the earliest days of Irish mythology."

"Since this tablet was left behind," Fred said. "That's good news."

Harry agreed. "The landmarks are the same now as they were then. What I'm hearing is you think I'm on to something."

Fred ignored him. "Another question. Why do these tablets exist? What purpose did they serve?"

"If I had to guess I'd say they tie in with the Romans invading Brittania."

"Based on the first tablet. That could be more evidence you're correct. It could also mean you should be worried."

"About what?"

"Collapsing bridges and crumbling tunnels are not left by accident. Those were meant to stop anyone other than true believers in the mythology from unraveling this mystery. Someone was very serious about protecting whatever it is this path reveals. Perhaps it is the Four Treasures. Perhaps not. Either way, the journey will be dangerous."

"Is there any other kind?" Harry quipped with a grin.

"The path and any obstacles on it must only prevail once. You must succeed again and again."

"I handled the first part. I can do this."

"I admire your confidence. I hope your caution is as strong." Fred never belabored a point. "Where is this Stone of Fal?"

"North of Kilkenny. I'm headed up there next."

"After you decipher the meaning of this new tablet."

Harry hesitated. "Yes."

"How?"

"Go to the Fal Stone and look for anything tied to Danu."

"You can do better than that. Break the message down now, piece by piece. What do you know already about Danu or her cross?"

Harry didn't grumble. His dad was right. "Not much."

"The odds are the Irishmen or women behind these messages wouldn't lean just on the written word. Their primary means of passing information was oral. Look for tangible objects that existed in pre-Roman times. Perhaps part of the geography, or something left behind as a marker. Something others have missed. Now, tell me about Danu."

"Danu is akin to a leader of the Tuatha, though not much is known about her. Most of the stories focus on other gods in their pantheon. It seems Danu led the other gods, but didn't rule them. She's associated with the earth and its bounties, how it sustains all life." Harry stopped to consider. "What sustains life on earth?"

"Now you're asking good questions."

"How do you know?"

"They're the ones I would ask."

Fair enough. "The sun sustains life," Harry said. "Maybe this has something to do with the sun."

"I suggest you get to the Fal Stone early. When the sun first touches the world. Go there when it's dark, reconnoiter the area and see if you identify any possibilities for the four-sided question. Do that and you'll be ready for the morning."

"When I'll have to move quickly," Harry said. "Whatever message sunrise brings won't be there long."

"Don't forget to consider different angles to the story. Try to understand the entire picture. It's not enough that I think you're on the right course. Odds are we both missed a piece of the puzzle. What else is tied in to this path?"

Harry hazarded a guess. "Romans? The treasures?"

"Start there. Research the treasures as much as you can. Then look at the Roman angle. Why did the Romans want these treasures? Not for money. They had enough of that."

The Roman Republic had existed in a near-constant state of warfare, much of it successful, which led to incredible expansion over the centuries. Maintaining control of the people in a conquered land within these new borders was a challenge, one at which the Romans excelled.

"The Romans wanted these treasures because they represented power and authority to the conquered people," Harry said.

"How so?"

The Four Treasures were central pillars of the faith of the ancient Irish, and Harry told his dad that. "Controlling these treasures would legitimize the Romans. Over time it could make the Irish more likely to accept the Romans' rule."

"Agreed," Fred said. "Though the Irish would never forget that the treasures were stolen. What could change is the perception surrounding those treasures, the perception of what they represented."

"I'm not following you."

"The treasures symbolize Irish beliefs, along with the ceremonies and shared customs honoring those beliefs. What was the most sacred ceremony in early Ireland?"

Harry wracked his brain and thankfully didn't come up empty. "The Midsummer celebration."

"Correct."

Harry should long ago have given up being surprised at what his dad knew. "How did you know that?"

"I took more than a few history classes. I remember things."

Harry rolled his eyes at the inside joke. "Thanks. About Midsummer?"

"Midsummer was the central pagan celebration."

"The summer solstice. A religion that worships nature would revere the day of the year with the most sunlight."

"A list that includes Hinduism, Buddhism and a host of other faiths. Danu is tied to the sun in the beliefs of the Irish and on your tablet." Fred paused. "Most importantly, it's a celebration that thrives even today. Every Christian celebrates it."

"Christians?" Harry tried to interrupt but Fred was having none of it. His dad could lecture with the best of them.

"I'm getting ahead of myself," Fred went on, ignoring Harry's question. "The Christians weren't the first to do it."

"To do what?"

"Steal the holiday. Or reappropriate it, if you prefer."

And with that, it all made sense. "That's why they wanted the treasures," Harry said.

"Seems like they failed," Fred said. "But when did truth ever get in the way of good cultural theft? The Romans didn't get the treasures, but they did get their holiday. Which they turned from an Irish myth into a Roman event. The Festival of the Goddess Fortuna."

Whose name Harry recognized. "That was the Midsummer celebration in Rome," he said, then paused as a thought called for attention. "Hold on. Wasn't Fortuna stolen—sorry, *reappropriated*—from a Greek deity?"

"You mean the Greek goddess Tyche. Whom the Romans took as their own god by giving her a new name and a fresh coat of paint. Well done, Harry."

"A central Irish pagan holiday first went to the Romans, then on to Christians." Harry waited for an explanation.

"Rome's Fortuna's festival was recast by early Christians as Saint John's Day. Today European celebrations include Saint John's fires being lit as part of the festivities. Big fires."

"Sounds an awful lot like how Irish pagans would have celebrated Midsummer."

"It certainly does. Fire and the sun tie together. You would be well served to see what else you can learn about the Midsummer observance before sunrise tomorrow."

"I'm working on it," Harry said. "And then I'll read through the history of the Four Treasures again."

"You never know what part of the Four Treasures legend matters to your search," Fred said. "I've learned that."

Fred Fox likely knew more about locating ancient relics than almost anyone in the world. Not because he had a fanatical desire to retrieve cultural objects or knowledge, though he did enjoy it, but because he did it for the pay, and he was very good. "Did you tell Mr. Morello about this?" Harry asked.

"No. You don't work for him." Fred rarely raised his voice or spoke harshly, but those words carried. "This is yours. Only yours."

Harry didn't argue with his father, at least not often, and never with Vincent Morello. Not many people argued with Vincent, a decent man who loved Harry's father for reasons Harry didn't fully understand, and who employed Fred Fox as his personal relic hunter. The fact Vincent Morello was the *capo dei capi* of New York's five families also had something to do with hardly anyone disagreeing with him. Smart people shied away from conflict with the boss of all bosses in New York. "I won't let you down," Harry said.

"You never do. Now, tell me your plan."

"Read up on the Four Treasures and the Midsummer celebration. As a pagan, Roman and Christian holiday. Then be at the Fal Stone before daybreak to find anything with four sides."

"Why not go there now? Survey the grounds before the sun goes down, then do your research."

A dog on a leash came over to sniff at Harry's boots. The owner took one look at his mud-stained pants and pulled the dog back. "Not a bad idea," Harry said as the dog owner crossed the street and narrowly avoided a man pushing a keg of beer on a handcart. He consulted his watch. "It's ninety minutes to the Stone. I need to move."

"I'm here if you want to talk," Fred said. "I believe in you."

Harry hesitated as he stood. "Thanks, Dad."

He clicked off and stuck the phone in his pocket. Five minutes later he was behind the wheel of his rental car with a hot coffee in the cupholder, and slightly less than ninety minutes of responsibly breaking the speed limit later he turned into a parking lot near a visitor center. The Fal Stone was the most prominent artifact on this Irish historical site known as the Hill of Tara. The site had endured since the Stone Age, first as a burial ground for notable men whose names had been lost to history, then in the five-hundred-year period around the time of Christ when it was known as the seat of the High King of Ireland. What made it so enduring? The Fal Stone.

How the Fal Stone came to stand on this hill was a mystery. Other objects of historical interest were also at the site. There was a towering Celtic cross, and an old castle that had partially fallen down but still loomed large; there was also a large burial mound covered in the greenest of Irish grass that Harry could see as he stepped out of his car. At one point this had been the figurative center of pagan Ireland. The place to which all roads steeped in mythology led. A place, he hoped, that still held tightly to at least one secret from the past.

Harry chased his shadow up the verdant hillside as he jogged toward the Fal Stone. The sun's lower rim was just touching the horizon when he reached the Stone, which rose well above his head. One side of the stone was covered in imagery. Not Latin letters, but drawings of animals, buildings, weapons and symbols of nature. Clouds and rivers, the sun and the moon. Put together, they made zero sense. Why cover the stone with these images? The choices had to serve a purpose.

The sun fell quickly. Harry had barely finished inspecting the symbols before the light was nearly gone, and with it, the park's visiting hours. The last thing he needed was to get run out of there by a park employee who would remember his face. He turned to look at the castle ruins. Ruins that could have inspired Ireland's own Bram Stoker, the novelist who had brought Count Dracula into the world. Dracula's castle sort of looked like this one, Harry mused.

He shook his head. Focus, Harry. He turned away from the castle. He stopped. *Interesting.*

Night fell as he stood beside the Fal Stone for a long minute, thinking; then he turned as he spied a pair of headlights coming down the road. He knew they might belong to the Irish version of a park ranger, so he took one final look at what had his eye before turning and heading for his car, his mind churning. Perhaps the answer had been in front of him all along. Only one way to know for sure. Get back here before dawn. Then watch the goddess Danu rise.

Chapter 3

*D*ublin, Ireland

"We have a problem."

Thomas O'Malley paused with the cup of tea halfway to his lips. He set it down and stared at the cell phone on his desk. "What sort of problem?"

The response that came back echoed, as though the person speaking was standing in an enclosed area. "Someone found a new tunnel in Dunmore Cave."

"When?"

"I'm working on that."

"Jonny, you said this is a problem." Tom O'Malley drummed his fingers on the desktop. "An empty cave is not a problem. What is in the cave?"

Tom listened as Jonny described a collapsed bridge, broken tunnel walls and three stone pillars. Or what remained of the pillars, at least. "We won't know the full story until engineers find a way to cross the pit," Jonny said. "I got as close as I could and used my binoculars."

Tom resisted the urge to tell Jonny to find a way across, and find it now. "What else was in the tunnel?"

"A handle of some kind was hanging from the cave roof over the pit. And one pillar that didn't fall down looked like something was burned on top of it."

"We've checked that cave a dozen times," Tom said. "I did it once myself. What did we miss?"

Tom O'Malley looked out the window of his Dublin office. A steady stream of car traffic moved up and down the city street. Pedestrians moved with purpose, most with their heads down, though some were enjoying the afternoon sunlight. None came inside the nondescript building housing the Irish Heritage Society, a fundraising arm tied to the governmental Office of Public Works, where they would have found an unremarkable office populated by average people. Most of those people truly did work on raising funds to assist in preserving sites of cultural importance in Ireland. Only a select few, however, carried out the Society's true mission. A mission led by Tom.

He turned away from the window. "Exactly when did you discover this new cave?" he asked.

"About an hour ago," Jonny said. "A hiker reported smelling smoke. I went in and found a hole in the wall that had been hidden behind stacked stones. There was a handle inside the hole. I pulled it, the wall opened, and suddenly there's a new tunnel."

"Do you have any idea who opened it?"

"Security cameras in the vicinity are being retrieved now. I wanted to call you first."

"Don't let anyone else see the tape," Tom said. "Take control of the site."

"Already done," Jonny said. "I'll have the footage any minute. Once I get a clear image of the person who was here, I'll call."

"Don't forget to check for their vehicle," Tom said. "A number plate could be better than a blurry photograph."

Tom clicked off. He did not get up. He picked up his tea and found it cold. The world around him seemed out of focus, background noise to the main event underway in his mind. Two thousand years. That's how long his people had been searching. For two millennia the men and women who came before Tom had worked to uncover the location of three objects. It was a search of faith as much as fact, for no one truly knew that the objects even existed.

Legend said the three objects had been secreted across Ireland for protection, meant to be recovered at the right time. All well and good, except the problem with any legend was nobody knew the truth and the stories changed over time. Little to nothing was written down. Details were lost through the years. Despite this, Tom and those who came before him never gave up hope, convinced that one day the objects would be found. The three lost treasures of the Tuatha Dé Danaan.

The Fal Stone existed. That fact kept the spark of hope alive that the remaining treasures were waiting to be found. Stories passed down from the earliest followers told of a tablet that would reveal the path for recovering the three hidden treasures. A tablet that had not been seen for two thousand years.

"Someone found it." Tom looked at his phone. "It's the only way." He grabbed his phone and dialed a number, waiting until a woman's voice answered. "Tom?"

"I have news. Are you alone?"

Lauren Brosnan said she was. "What's wrong?"

"Someone found the tablet."

"Found the—*what*?"

Tom detailed what he knew. Jonny was a Society member who monitored historical sites through his job with the Office of Public Works and could be trusted. "That's all I know now," Tom finished.

"Jonny is trying to locate anything on the person who found the new cave. A picture, a number plate. Anything."

"Let me help."

Lauren worked as a true fundraiser for their group. Her gift lay in connecting with people, in lighting a fire inside anyone so they felt the same passion she did for preserving Ireland's heritage. With passion came donations, and no one in the Society was better at their job than Lauren. She was a true believer. "I can help find whoever it is." She took a breath. "Just think, Tom. We could be close. We could prove it's all true."

It was more than the three ancient relics. Much more. "We can't do anything until we know who was there. How did they find the hidden cave? What was inside? Focus on that first. Then we find the person."

"Let me help you."

Her voice brooked no dissent. Tom could almost see the freckles on her cheeks heating up. "Of course I will," he said. The phone beeped. "Jonny's calling. Keep your phone close." Tom clicked over to Jonny's call. "What do you have?"

"Half a picture and a partial number plate. I just sent you the photo."

Tom's phone pinged and an image appeared on-screen. A man's face in profile as he walked between trees. Shadows made it difficult to get a clear view of his features. "He's not Irish," Tom said.

"His family may have immigrated," Jonny said.

The man's complexion wasn't quite dark enough to stand out, but was nothing like the light tone of most Irish. Perhaps English and Middle Eastern? The man's head of dark hair sat atop an athletic physique. "He's young," Tom said. "Mid-twenties at most."

"This is him leaving Dunmore Cave," Jonny said. "Here's another shot of him walking toward the cave."

"He's cleaner when he goes in," Tom said. "It looks as though he was dragged through dirt inside the cave."

"There's a third image." Another ping on Tom's phone. "This is the partial number plate. It shows the first few letters on his car, and we can identify the manufacturer. But that's not all. Zoom in on the man."

Tom studied an image taken from higher up, as though the camera was on a light pole. The camera aimed toward the parking lot, and though a tree partially blocked the view, Tom could make out several numbers on the back of a dark-colored sedan. Tom spread his fingers on the screen, enlarging the photo and showing the man beside the sedan. "I can't see his face."

"Look at his right arm."

Tom enlarged the image. "He's holding something." Tom peered at the slightly out-of-focus object for some time. "I can't make out what it is."

"I think he's holding a tablet," Jonny said. "What if that's what he found inside?"

"If you're right, this man has new information about our history. Lauren will help us get the full number plate. She has contacts."

"One more thing about the man," Jonny said. "I'm sending a video clip."

Tom waited for it to arrive. "It's his car leaving," Tom said. "But I still can't see the plate number or the man's face. It's too far away."

"Don't look for the man. Look at his car. At how he drives it. *Where* he drives it."

"He's on the wrong side of the road. He's driving–"

"–like an American."

Tom replayed the video. The car pulled out of the visitor center parking lot, turned onto the roadway, and drove for several seconds on the right side of the road. The side Americans drove on. He then quickly swerved to the left side, the British side for drivers, and continued. A small mistake. A telling one. "He's not British," Tom said. "Call me if you learn anything else about the caves or this man. And Jonny."

"Yes?"

"Don't tell anyone about this. No one at all. Understood?"

Jonny said he did and Tom cut the call, dialing Lauren's number. She answered at once. "Do you have contacts in the Department of Transport?" Tom asked.

"I do," Lauren said.

"Find out who owns this vehicle." Tom ratted off the partial number plate and a description of the car. "It's likely a rental. We have to know who rented it. It's possibly an American. I'm sending you a photo of him now."

"Is it the man from Dunmore Cave?" Lauren asked moments later. Tom said it was. "Where would he be going now?"

"I don't know." Tom hesitated. Should he tell Lauren about the tablet? Security dictated the fewer people who knew, the better, but he needed Lauren to succeed. "We think he took something from the cave," Tom said. "He may have found the tablet." He pushed on to cut off her barrage of questions. "The one we haven't found in two thousand years."

"Find this man and we'll find the answers. Call me when you have anything."

"What will you do if I get his name?"

What would he do? "Locate him." What did she expect? "Then learn what he knows. He found the secret entrance. In a cave our people inspected. We missed it, Lauren. If we missed that, what else did we miss? He can tell us." Tom eyes narrowed. "He *will* tell us."

"There may be another option."

Tom's finger stopped an instant before disconnecting the call. "What?"

"We don't have to force him to talk. How would we know anything he says is true?"

"This man found what we couldn't. It may be luck, or it may be skill, and I'd argue it doesn't matter. All we know is he's further along than we are."

"Which is why we must learn what he knows. What's your plan—to accost him in the street? Maybe take the tablet from him and demand answers? I think we should wait. And follow him closely."

Tom opened his mouth. Tom closed his mouth. He thought it through. "Agreed. See where he leads us."

"And move in when the time is right. At which point we'll know enough to ask the right questions. More to the point, we'll know what he's capable of."

"It's not a great idea," Tom said. "But it's not bad."

"It looks like I'm around his age. He's in my country. He won't even notice me."

"Out of the question." This time it was Tom's tone that brooked no dissent.

Lauren was having none of it. "Why not?"

"Because I said so. End of discussion. I'm in charge. Your task is to find this man's identity through the number plate. Call me when you do. You don't try to find this guy; you don't do anything but call me with the information. Understood?"

Lauren may have grumbled, but she was smart enough to make sure he didn't hear it.

"Listen." Tom sighed. "This is the chance we've been waiting for. Our Society is small. We're up against a much larger foe."

"The Irish government."

"Which, fortunately, has been convinced we may not even exist."

The Irish Heritage Society needed the three missing treasures to prove what they believed was right: that the Irish government and its elected representatives were not the sole leaders of Ireland. They all sat on stolen seats. And Tom and his Society needed the treasures to prove it.

"Locating the treasures is our goal," Tom said. "Do that and we can strengthen our claim by proving the Irish myths came first. Before Christianity."

"Everyone knows that."

"It doesn't matter what they know. It matters what we can do to inflame their passions. Ireland is a Christian nation, but if we remind people of the power and truth in Irish myths, we have a better chance of gaining support for our cause."

Lauren knew what was coming. "You mean Midsummer? That it's rooted in Ireland?"

"First the Romans stole it, and then the Christians. We need to remind the world of the true origins. We'll never win in their court of law."

Lauren understood. "But we can win in the court of public opinion. In Irish people's hearts. Drive their nationalism, their love for Ireland."

"Yes. Help me finish what our ancestors started. Get me the man's identity. I'll take it from there."

Lauren agreed and clicked off. Tom let out a long breath, and when he picked up his mug, he didn't go to the tea kettle. He opened a drawer in his desk and poured out a measure of whiskey. This work called for strong nerves. One nip from his favorite distillery would do the trick.

The whiskey, however, did little to still his thoughts. What if this man worked for someone? He could be tied to the Irish government. Tom frowned at that. Their enemies, the people running their country, might have the lead in this chase. Or the man could be employed by any number of other governments, or opposing organizations within Ireland.

"Stop it." He put his cup down. Speculating served no purpose. Identify the man and move on from there. Stay rational. Those were the sorts of thoughts he tried to bury the deepest. That his mission, his faith in the true myths from which Ireland was born, was all a lie. That perhaps they had never been true and had instead been created out of thin air to give credence to the original myths; that the Fal Stone where High Kings of Ireland had been crowned for centuries was nothing more than a rock dug from some charlatan's back yard.

Tom couldn't say how long he sat there, but the summer sun was still strong in the sky when his phone buzzed. Lauren was calling. "Did you find something?" he asked.

"I know who he is," she said quickly. "You're never going to believe it."

Chapter 4

County Meath, Ireland

Innumerable stars filled the fading night sky. The first hint of dawn touched the eastern horizon, though on the ground at the Hill of Tara night still reigned. A single pair of headlights pushed back against the dark as a car pulled into the visitor center parking lot. The headlights went out. The rumbling engine fell silent, and a moment later a flashlight beam cut across the damp grass as a man stood outside the car, looking ahead.

Harry Fox had arrived early. This protected cultural site didn't open until sunrise, so his arrival well ahead of that was a roll of the dice. He could always claim ignorance if anyone else showed up. He couldn't sit in his hotel room any longer with his entire nervous system firing at full speed. He'd spent half the night researching. What he learned had led him to one conclusion: he was on the right path.

The distant castle ruins were a black spot on the landscape, the old stones seeming to absorb all light they touched. Harry walked to the Fal Stone and studied the engravings, trying and failing to piece together any coherent message in the carvings. Forget that people a lot smarter than him had failed at that over the past two millennia. Now Harry had a resource they didn't. The second stone tablet.

Unable to make heads or tails of the stone imagery, he turned from the Fal Stone and headed for the castle. Harry cast only a short glance at the towering Celtic cross he passed on his route, facts and stories of ancient myth racing through his mind.

He knew Irish pagans, as the Christians later called them, celebrated the summer solstice with bonfires and feasting, raucous parties honoring the middle of summer, the season that brought them long days, shorter nights and abundant warmth. A joyous occasion, though the Irish couldn't have foreseen what would come about because of those festivals.

The Romans had come calling. That empire's insatiable appetite for expansion had led to the first incursion onto Irish soil by a Roman when the Governor of Brittania sent an expedition into his territory. Last night Harry had learned that a man named Gnaeus Julius Agricola led this first invasion. Agricola was known to history as the man who conquered Brittania, serving as the governor as he probed the outer reaches of his territory, venturing into but never subduing Ireland.

Rome never conquered Ireland, but that didn't mean the Irish escaped Roman influence. Romans claimed Irish pagan celebrations as part of their own religion, appropriating the Midsummer celebration and calling it the Festival of the Goddess Fortuna. Christianity later did the same by recasting the holiday as Saint John's Day. But in Brittania, the Romans undermined Midsummer completely. They knew that to conquer a people required more than simple military might. It also required capturing hearts and minds. How better to do this than by co-opting a religious day, merging the new with the old to make bending the knee more palatable?

Agricola understood this, which is why Harry believed the Governor of Brittania tried to steal the Four Treasures to use as his own symbols of the holiday. Keep the peace and keep the Irish tax revenue flowing. Do that, and Agricola had won.

"Nothing is so secure as that money will not defeat it." Harry grinned without humor at the old quote. "True today and true then." Roman money hadn't conquered Ireland, but it had stolen their cultural treasure. Midsummer belonged to the descendants of those pagan citizens. Maybe it was time to bring those treasures back into the light and to the true owners.

Harry stopped walking. He leaned back and looked up. His flashlight beam ran up and down the towering castle walls, slipping through holes in the exterior stones and through long-empty windows. The partially ruined castle in front of him resembled a place Count Dracula might call home. A chill ran up Harry's spine. *I'll wait to go in there when the sun comes up.*

Which wouldn't be long. He studied the castle exterior for a moment longer, looking for something—he wasn't sure what. Maybe he'd be back. Maybe not. It depended on what happened behind him when the sun rose. He turned and studied the lightening sky, the stars becoming a memory, the black sky turning purple with a touch of blue at its edges. Harry walked with purpose toward his true destination. The Celtic cross.

Born in Ireland, this ringed cross added a circle running around the intersection of the vertical and horizontal beams of a traditional Christian cross. The version erected on this hill dated to the same time period as the Fal Stone. If the Celtic cross had gone up at the same time as the Fal Stone, they could be connected.

The cross was on a low rise in the hillside, its base lower in elevation than the base of the Fal Stone. Harry stood so the cross was between him and the Stone. He reached up as far as he could, his hand almost touching the point where the two cross beams intersected in the circle.

He looked around. No one else had yet arrived. He stepped onto the base of the cross, which lifted him up enough so he could reach above the intersecting portions.

He held onto the vertical beam with one hand, held his flashlight in the other, and leaned back as far as he could before holding the flashlight up and shining it directly through the circle. He looked ahead and his eyes widened. *I was right.*

The Celtic cross cut his flashlight beam into four pieces. Each spot of light shifted in tandem with the others as he struggled to keep his balance, four dots chasing each other over the wet grass. He adjusted the light so it raced further up the hill toward the summit. What he saw sent him leaping off the cross's base before he turned to look behind him, to the east, where the horizon had brightened to a soft red line across the world that would soon explode with sunlight. He checked his watch. Less than a minute. He ran toward the top of the hill.

The sky changed quickly. Harry blinked and the soft purple blanket turned to soft blue as the sun peeked over the horizon. He shielded his eyes as the sun appeared directly behind the tall Celtic cross and threw a long shadow up the hillside, one that directly covered the Fal Stone as it grew. Four dots of light crept from the ground in front of the Celtic cross and moved toward the Fal Stone. He looked to the Stone and the images carved on it, trying to predict what would happen.

The four dots of sunlight reached the stone's base. Harry leaned closer as the sun warmed his face. He reached into a pocket and grabbed a piece of chalk. The dots traveled up the Fal Stone, moving past the carvings. They skirted every carving they passed, touching the edges of some while slipping past others entirely. He didn't blink, didn't breathe. The world narrowed to those four dots as he watched them move up the ancient stone without illuminating a single carving.

Until they did. A message came alive.

Harry touched his chalk to the stone beside each highlighted image. The sun stayed on them for no more than two beats, then moved, the message only a memory. The four dots of light reached the stone's upper edge and then fell over it and out of sight. He put the chalk down and stepped back. What in the world did that mean?

Four images had been marked by the light. A ladder, a tower of some type, what looked like a horizon, and a shovel. He snapped a photo of the marked images with his phone and then rubbed the chalk marks away. How was this meant to be read? Irish pagans had little in the way of written records. Given that Latin had been the predominant written language of the time, should he assume these writings were meant to be read left to right, as if written in Latin? At least that gave him something to start with. "The first one is a ladder." A pair of longer vertical lines connected by four shorter, horizontal lines. "Maybe I'm supposed to climb something."

Next was what looked like a tower. This image, a vertical tube, was rendered with depth, almost three-dimensional. A small cutout in the tube's center near the top resembled a window, while up-and-down lines at the top made him think of crenellations along upper defensive walls of a castle.

Castle. Harry looked away from the Stone, across the green hillside now bathed in warm light, and toward the half-ruined structure. A formerly towering pile of stones. "Is that it?"

The castle hadn't fallen completely down. Far from it. In fact, part of the castle was in use as a visitor center. A building that stood slightly away from the main castle structure had been updated with modern windows and electric lighting to house attendants who oversaw the site. Harry looked at the highest part of the castle walls. To a tower, round like the image. He looked at the single window high up on the tall tower. A window centered on the rounded walls. A window with a partial wall above it. "It's crenellated. That's part of the message"

The sound of an approaching motor filled the air. A pair of head-lights appeared above a short rise in the distance, fell below the horizon, then reappeared as the sound of the whining engine grew louder. For a reason he couldn't name Harry hit the ground. His gut told him this car could be trouble. The car rounded a curve and came fully into view with the sun behind it, the sharp angle of the bright light making the car a dark outline. The driver slowed as they passed the visitors' parking lot. The engine noise lowered, the old brakes squealed, and as Harry was thinking about popping up and trying to act nonchalant, the engine came alive and the car puttered on.

Harry kept low until the noise faded from hearing. Maybe it was someone on a drive wondering what the park contained, or maybe peering at the stone and deciding a hunk of rock wasn't worth a stop. He got up from the ground. It seemed the Irish pagans had left more than one safeguard behind to protect whatever it was they wanted to hide. The Four Treasures? He could only hope.

The Fal Stone would be one of them and would serve two purposes. One, to show at least one treasure was more than myth. Two, to reveal the path to one deemed worthy of following it. He turned to face the crenellated tower that bore more than a passing resemblance to the tower on the Fal Stone. The upper reaches of the tower were at least thirty feet above ground level. It would take one heck of a ladder to climb that. Unless he took the tower stairs.

His boots left dark prints in the damp grass as he walked toward the tower. The attached visitor center wouldn't be open yet, and he couldn't imagine the crumbling tower section was open to the public. A towering wooden door turned black with age blocked anyone from entering through the front. Thick iron bars secured the wood boards that themselves looked hard as stone. The crumbled masonry to one side, however, offered much easier access.

Harry stood below a large hole in the castle wall. The stones looked like they had collapsed centuries ago. A patchwork attempt to support them was apparent from the more modern building material under the stones. Stones bigger than his head, some the size of his torso. Stones that would crush him flat if they came loose. He reached for the opening and came up inches short. Rather than jump straight up and risk bouncing off the wall, he took a few steps back and then ran at full speed toward the stone wall, leaping up and kicking off the stones to propel himself high enough to latch onto the lower lip of the opening with both hands. He pulled his body up as he flew, the momentum carrying him high enough to get his arms entirely through the opening. He didn't try to pull himself through to the inside of the castle. No telling what was inside or how much of a drop waited. He paused, his arms hanging over the lip and his head now high enough to see inside.

Dark shadows filled the interior. Dim light coming through holes in the castle roof lit dirty stone floors. He blinked, peering into the darkness at nothing but vague outlines as his eyes adjusted to the dim light. Both feet found crevices in the stonework to keep him aloft as the room came into view.

A car door slammed shut not far away.

Harry dropped from the window and hit the ground, crouching down to shelter against the castle wall. Voices came from the parking lot. Harry poked his head out around a bulging stone. Two people stood beside a car parked next to his.

One of those two people now pointed at Harry.

Chapter 5

Hill of Tara, County Meath

"I think he's hurt. Come on, let's check."

The shouted words were clear as day. Harry stayed tucked behind the castle wall, out of sight of the two people who'd just pulled into the parking lot and now seemed to think Harry had fallen from the castle windowsill and injured himself. He couldn't run for it. There was nothing but open grass all around. These two might be officials, the sort of people who wouldn't take kindly to him climbing around the castle. Footsteps grew louder as they approached him.

"Hello." Harry popped up from behind the outcropping, casually wiping nonexistent dirt from his pants.

A man and a woman stopped not five feet away. "Are you injured?" the man asked. "We saw you fall."

"Only my pride," Harry joked. "Slipped when I tried to see what was in there. I thought I heard something inside." Harry pointed at the window as though it weren't clear he meant the castle.

"You must have heard the spirits."

Harry stopped brushing. "The what?"

This time the woman answered. "The sacred spirits. The gods and goddesses who watch over this land." She spread her arms. The accent told Harry she likely hailed from this country. "You should listen to them when they speak."

Harry fought the urge to take a step back. "Right. Not sure if that's what I heard inside." He pointed at the castle again. "You guys ever go inside there?"

Both of them ignored his question until the man spoke. "The spirits communicate in many ways." Now the man inclined his head toward the big door. "The door is kept locked. The spirits and gods may move about this place, but we do not."

"Because the gods don't like it?" Harry hazarded.

The man smiled. "Trespassing is forbidden. Have you come here to worship?"

It hit him. They were *druids*. Or pagans, or neopagans, or whatever this iteration of Irish believers called themselves. "Nope," Harry said. "I'm here for the history."

The man gave Harry a slight bow. "Do not let us disturb you. We come to offer food and drink to the spirits of these lands. We honor them."

"I'll stay out of your way," Harry said.

The woman spun around to face him. "You are welcome everywhere," she said. "Unless you do not come in peace."

"I'm a peaceful guy. It's nice to meet you."

Harry pretended to be fascinated by the castle's exterior wall as he moved away from the two pagans, who seemed content to sing softly as they walked back toward their car. Harry moved slowly until he made it around a corner of the castle and was hidden from view. There had to be another way to get inside. This castle wall was as much hole as wall. Another window, or maybe a section of crumbled stone. He moved past the corner to the flat side wall. He stopped. "That could work."

Another empty window looked down on him from twenty feet in the air. Too high to jump, but the wall beneath was badly deteriorated, and a giant crevice ran from the ground to nearly the height of the window. *I can climb that.*

Climb to the windowsill, pull himself up, and he'd be in. Then a short walk to the crenellated tower. Nothing to it. As long as no park rangers or authorities showed up. Lifting himself up to peer into the castle was one thing. Traipsing around a clearly unsafe structure that might further damage said national treasure was another. The Irish wouldn't take kindly to that.

Waiting around only gave the authorities more time to show up. The jagged crack in the castle wall held firm when he grabbed hold, stuck a foot in and started climbing. Pebbles came loose, but the big stones held enough for Harry to hoist himself skyward. Ten feet above ground he fought the urge to look down. Not that a fall from here would hurt him. It was losing concentration that mattered. Secure holds, keep going. He kept his eyes straight ahead as he moved, one hand and foot after the other, until he could grab the lower lip of the windowsill and look through it.

"That's not good."

The window opened to the second level of the castle ruins. A large room with a mostly intact fireplace, and a ceiling overhead with holes here and there. Not bad for being a thousand years old. That was the good part. The bad? The floor beneath this window had vanished. Only a giant hole to the ground floor. Twenty feet down, then solid stone. Fall and who knows how he'd land. He couldn't leap across the hole. He'd have to jump at least ten feet straight out to get to the closest section of intact floor. A floor in which he had little faith could hold him.

The roof above him had held, and it included an iron monstrosity of a chandelier. Its central ring was larger than a dining room table and hung from iron rungs that looked like they came from a large ship's anchor chain. The chandelier hung directly over the hole in the floor. Harry studied it. "Looks sturdy." It had to be, if he wanted to get across this gap.

Even if he fell it was under twenty feet. He'd be fine. Hopefully only a twisted ankle. Then the thought of this giant chandelier coming down on top of him entered his mind, and he pushed it away just as quickly. No need to be negative. His arms protested as he pulled himself up to stand on the window ledge. He could get hold of the iron ring by leaping five feet at best, then start swinging and get the momentum to launch himself over the gap to the far side.

He crouched, flexed his fingers. A bird cried, and Harry jumped.

Got it. Rusty iron shouted as he latched onto the section of ring between two candleholders, his weight pushing the whole structure sharply forward. He kicked his feet to push it even more, then swung his feet back so the ring groaned and came thundering back toward the window. Stones cracked and the massive wooden ceiling beam to which the chandelier was attached rumbled as Harry swung backwards, then forward again, waiting until the last second on that forward swing before he jerked his body from head to toe as though a spasm had overtaken him, and in one final push, he let go of the iron ring and flew feet-first to land on the intact floor.

His feet hit the floor and shot out from under him so his upper back smacked the ground, the impact sending him tumbling out of control across the broken stone floor, the world twisting and turning until he crashed into a stone pillar and went still in a cloud of dust.

He blinked the dust from his eyes. Harry lay chest down with his head hanging over a second hole in the floor he hadn't known existed.

If he had rolled a few more feet, he would have fallen through. He narrowed his gaze. Fallen through to land directly onto chunks of stone. "Those look sharp."

Harry pulled himself back from the precipice and stood. Chunks were missing from the floor in random places. It looked like anywhere that had a supporting arch on the lower level should be safe, however, so he went cautiously across the remaining floor, past multiple fireplaces big enough to park a car in, until he reached the staircase leading to the far tower. A tower with only one window.

His gut told him to look out that single window. He climbed the stairs and did so, finding a view of rounded green hills on two sides of a much larger rise in the terrain. He couldn't miss the connection. The waving line highlighted on the Fal Stone had shown two shorter, rounded lines on either side of a narrower, taller line. "It's that hillside," Harry said. "That's where the stone points."

A ladder, the tower, now the hillside. The only remaining image from the Fal Stone was a shovel. "I need to get to that tall hill. And I need a shovel." He almost turned, then stopped. "Where am I supposed to dig?"

The hillside wasn't massive, but it was expansive enough that he could spend a long time digging in the wrong places. There had to be a sign here somewhere showing him where to start. He rubbed the back of his neck. *Think. The answer is here.*

He stopped rubbing his neck and went still. "No way."

The opening in front of him would once have contained glass panes, so there was a narrow ledge into which the glass would have been secured. The center support stone on this now empty ledge had a carving.

The carving was an exact image of the terrain outside this window. With one addition. The carving had a small Celtic cross, placed slightly to the left side of the highest peak ahead. "That's where I dig."

He snapped a photo of the ledge image and backtracked to the gaping hole beneath the chandelier. He didn't need to get back across the hole to the far edge. He only needed to get down.

It took a moment to steel his nerves before he knelt and slid on this stomach until he was over the edge, dangling above the floor below. He looked for a soft landing spot. Nothing presented itself. More than ten feet separated the bottom of his boots from the floor below. One handhold shifted as part of a stone came loose and dropped. Hard to ignore a sign from the gods. He let go.

The floor rushed up to meet him. Harry tried to tuck and roll, failed miserably, and for the second time that day he crashed onto a stone floor. This time he came up with an aching shoulder. Harry cursed himself silently as he limped out through a previously unseen opening in the outside wall and felt the wonderfully soft grass below his feet. He brushed himself off, stiffened his back, and walked around the corner trying to look as though he had not just committed several crimes.

The pair of druids he'd encountered earlier were in the parking lot and they'd made two new friends. Another man and woman stood talking to them. Harry kept his head down and went directly to his car parked on the other side of the lot. He paused to tie his shoe, getting a good look at the new people, or as good a look as he could from a hundred feet away. None of the four seemed interested as he walked to his car, popped the trunk, and pulled out a small pack he had assembled for his search back in Dunmore Cave. He hadn't needed it there, but he did now.

He opened the pack, checked everything was in order, then slung it over his shoulder and set off. It held climbing rope, a folding military shovel, and a small electric lantern along with a few other tools. Now, to find the cross. Do that first and figure out the rest later.

He hiked toward the rising hills and ran through the clue again. The Celtic cross carving was a marker showing where to look and dig. The sun had fully risen by the time he covered the quarter mile to begin climbing the long central hill. He picked up the pace and headed for the western side of the hill, which would put the parking lot out of view and partially hide him from anyone at the visitor center.

Harry looked back before the parking lot vanished and saw the two druids kneeling in front of the Fal Stone, while the other two were inspecting the castle by the spot where Harry had broken in. He crested a slight rise and then dipped out of sight, hidden for the moment. A copse of trees stood on either side. The hillside sloped down to his left, while it rose to a somewhat rounded peak several hundred feet up the hill to his right. He stood roughly where the Celtic cross had been depicted on the window ledge. Nothing stood out.

He continued walking. The grass now reached partway up his shins; this area was less maintained than the central portion of the site. Other than a spot to one side of him. A spot right along the ridgeline, maybe twenty feet up. He veered off and ascended the hillside until he was standing on a what had looked like a patch of bare ground that, on closer inspection, wasn't so bare. No grass grew due to the large stone in the ground. A square stone with edges that he wouldn't call natural. A passing cloud blocked the sunlight and sent a shadow across the stone.

"There's a carving on it." He knelt to run his hands over the stone. The imprint had been worn by time to nearly nothing. He lay flat on his stomach and looked across the stone from ground level. He recognized the image once carved into this stone. A *Celtic cross.*

The cross was identical to the cross he'd seen in the castle. With the terrain largely protecting him from view, he dropped his pack to the ground and pulled out the shovel. Harry rested the pointed tip on the ground and stopped. Where to dig first? He couldn't very well break the stone. Above it? To one side?

He stepped on the shovel and plunged it into the dirt beside the stone, lifting a clump of earth up and dumping it beside him. Another shovelful came up, his blade scraping the stone as he worked. Shovel, scrape, dump. Five times he repeated the process. The dirt pile beside him grew rapidly. What was he going to do with all the dirt? It was a calling card asking any passersby to investigate. He lifted another shovelful, dumped it, and jammed the shovel back into the ground.

Clank.

Bolts of pain raced up each arm to rattle his molars. Another rock must be adjacent to this stone marker. Harry twisted the shovel around and used the point as a trowel to scrape away at the thin layer of dirt covering whatever had just brought this dig to a screeching halt.

Another, harsher, scraping sound. He stopped. "That's not stone—it's iron."

The rusted top layer of the iron flaked as he dragged the shovel tip over it. The deep red color of the metal stood out against the much darker earth. A shape emerged as he scraped more dirt away. "An iron ring."

The ring was attached directly to the side of the stone beneath the cross carving. The ring was roughly the size of a dinner plate and bolted to the stone marker. He kept scraping, clearing dirt from around the entire stone. Nothing but dirt turned up along both sides.

The ring seemed to have no purpose. He couldn't very well lift the entire stone. What *was* this?

Dong. His shovel hit another hunk of rusted iron. Not a ring this time. "It's some kind of hinge."

A rusted iron hinge buried partway along the edge of the stone came into view, situated opposite the ring. Harry dug closer to the far edge of the stone. "Found you," he said when his shovel clanged again. A second hinge.

"It opens." Harry finished digging out this rear side and stepped back. He wiped sweat from his eyes. "If the ring is a handle, then this stone moves on hinges."

Harry stopped digging and stepped around to stand in front of the ring. He bent low, grabbed it with both hands, and pulled.

No dice. He grunted, cursed, sweated and struggled. One second, the stone lay flat. The next, a screeching sound of tortured iron that definitely roused a few corpses in the nearby graves cut the air, and he heaved the stone upright. The Celtic cross rose up as he threw the stone back so it stood upright on the hinges. Harry stared at what lay beneath.

Narrow stairs descending into the darkness of the sloping hill.

Chapter 6

Hill of Tara, County Meath

"He's disappeared."

Tom O'Malley's head appeared next to hers. "What do you mean, disappeared?"

Lauren Brosnan stood next to her and Tom's car as she pointed at the hillside ahead of them. "He walked over that hill," she said. "I can't see him."

This was the second time she'd lost sight of Harry Fox. Lauren and Tom had arrived at Tor Hill's visitor parking lot a half hour earlier to find two cars on site, but only one group of visitors. Harry Fox had been nowhere in sight, so they'd approached the couple standing by the Fal Stone who turned out to be druids. Had they seen anyone here today? Why yes, they had, but they'd lost track of him. Nice young man. Didn't look like he was from around here. He'd asked about the castle ruins. Was Lauren here to honor the gods?

Lauren had thanked the couple and managed to keep a neutral face as she turned away. This was impossible. Her contact in the Department of Transport had provided Harry Fox's rental car information, and Lauren had called in other favors to track the rental car, using its internal GPS, to this parking lot. That same car sat not a hundred feet away. He couldn't hide around here. Gentle hills stretched out in every direction. Nobody could simply walk off and vanish.

Lauren had been on the verge of screaming when Harry stumbled out from behind the castle ruins. She took a breath, let it out, then touched Tom's shoulder. "I see him," she'd said.

"What was he doing in the castle?" Tom had asked before shaking his head. "Keep an eye on him. He can't get far without his car. We'll stay up here."

A conservative plan. Not the one Lauren would have decided on, but Tom was the boss. She knew Harry hadn't crossed an ocean and trekked through the Dunmore Caves for nothing. This man had a purpose. He had now found a trail, a path no one else had located. Pretty impressive, except Harry Fox now stood between her organization and the solution to a millennia-old mystery. She'd have been impressed if she weren't so busy worrying.

"I can't just stay here." She rapped a finger on the car hood. "He might leave another way."

"And go where?" Tom gestured all around to make his point. "There's nothing nearby. He'll come back."

Lauren's voice dropped. "Those two druids told us he was asking about the castle and the cross. Something about one of those things has his attention." She tapped the car hood again. "This guy isn't a regular American tourist. Not even close."

She had done a double-take when her government contacts ran a background search for her. They'd used the partial plate and car description from surveillance cameras outside Dunmore Caves, which led to a man named Harry Fox, who had rented the vehicle. Lauren had done her due diligence, and that's when she'd discovered the truth. Harry Fox was more than just an overzealous tourist from Brooklyn.

Tom waved a dismissive hand. "So his father may have ties to organized crime. What does that matter? Half the people in Brooklyn do. He could be an accountant for all we know."

The report had told Lauren only that Harry Fox's father was suspected of having ties to New York's biggest gangster. "Vincent Morello is not a man to trifle with," she said.

"Then don't tell this Fox guy your real name," Tom said. "We'll ask questions. He'll give us answers. Then he goes back to Brooklyn and we carry on. End of story."

Her jaw clenched. She let it go. "Understood," she said. "I still don't like sitting here. I want to see what he's doing. I won't approach him. Just watch." She let Tom chew on that for a full minute. "Tom, there's no reason we can't walk toward the woods. Anyone can go there."

"You're not going to drop this, are you?" Tom asked. Lauren assured him she was not. "Fine. On one condition." Tom raised a finger. "Do not approach him. I do the talking."

"Agreed." She waited for an appropriate length of time. "What if he found it already?"

"Found what?"

"That's what I'm trying to figure out," Lauren said. "Which we cannot do standing in this parking lot."

Tom grumbled. "Come on." He walked toward the hillside without waiting for her. "Better than standing around listening to you complain."

Lauren did not try to hide her grin as they walked. They gave the two overly friendly druids a wide berth as they passed the Celtic cross. The light breeze flicked at her hair, and Lauren found herself well ahead of Tom as they began descending a sloping hillside that hopefully would bring Harry Fox into view.

"Slow down," Tom said.

Lauren turned to look at Tom after he spoke. "We have no idea what he's doing," she replied.

"What he'll be doing is getting suspicious of two people running up his backside," Tom said. "We're supposed to be out for a stroll. Act like it."

She waited for him to catch up. "You're awfully calm for a man who might render our organization obsolete."

Tom stopped. "What on earth does that mean?"

"Our Irish Heritage Society has existed in one form or another for two thousand years. With one driving goal."

"I'm aware," Tom said.

She carried on as though he hadn't responded. "To locate the Four Treasures and empower the return of our beliefs. The treasures will prove the Irish government is not the sole leader of our land. There is another leader. A *true* leader."

"I admire your passion." Tom kept his pace slow as they reached the bottom of the small gulley. "Yes, the treasures will prove our claim." He glanced back toward where they'd passed the Fal Stone. "Perhaps we will return here soon."

"We have a right to govern ourselves as a people," she said. "There is a rightful leader of this land and we must make that known. With the treasures as the proof."

"I know," Tom said. "The seat of power was stolen." He hesitated. "At least that's what we've been told."

The ground sloped upward as they walked. "What we've been told?" Lauren asked. "It's true." She stopped walking. "Isn't it?"

Tom stopped beside her and put his hands on his hips. "The people who told our legends believed it was true."

Her eyes widened. "You don't?"

Tom ran a hand over his face. "Sometimes I'm not sure what I believe. Two thousand years without a single piece of evidence. At times I worry these are stories, tales passed down over time, with the truth slipping away over the years."

She'd never heard him talk this way. "If they're not true, then why are we here?"

"Because we believe. Are we right? I can't say for certain." Now his voice hardened and he pointed back the way they'd come. "The Fal Stone exists. It's a treasure of our ancestors. I'm certain of that. And if it exists, then I believe the other treasures are real. I believe we are led by a false government." He touched his chest. "I have faith, even as I have some doubt. I have faith in our stories and our people. People like you."

Lauren looked at Tom O'Malley as though he were a new man. "I've never heard you speak that way," she said. Tom didn't respond. "You know we're doing it for everyone," Lauren said. "All the people being ignored by our government."

"The government is very good at ignoring anyone they label pagans." Tom's tone darkened. "They want to erase our history. To them, Christianity is all that matters now. Pagan history is vilified."

"It's not right," Lauren said. "Our history is Ireland's history. We all deserve a seat at the table."

"Perhaps more than that," Tom said. "One day."

He fell silent as they moved up the hill until they could see over the top and into the distance. They both stopped. Lauren spoke first. "He's not around here."

A new hill rose in front of them, this one slightly taller, with an even higher one beyond that. They'd have to walk down a small valley and up the larger hill to see what lay beyond. Doing so would take them roughly a half-mile from the site. "He could be somewhere beyond this hill," Lauren said.

"What could take him so far from the main site?" Tom looked around again as though they could have missed Harry. "There are trees over on that hill. They could be hiding him. He could be looking at us right now."

"Then we'd better keep moving," Lauren said. "No need to stand here looking suspicious."

The leafy tops of trees could be seen fluttering just above the horizon as they climbed. One grouping to either side. Lauren's steps quickened as they approached the summit of the hill, with the peak of the tallest hill on the other side. Her shoes rustled in the grass as she reached the upper limit of the first hill and peered over the top.

"Stop." Lauren threw a hand out and pulled Tom back down the slope. She kept still, then straightened slowly, only high enough that her eyes rose above the rounded top of the hill. "I see him," she said. "There's a short downslope ahead of us, then the ground rises again. A set of trees are on either side of the hill. Harry Fox is between them. He's digging."

"Digging?"

She looked down at him long enough to send her message. "A hole, Tom. He's digging a hole."

"Why?"

"I have no idea why." Two clanging noises sounded, the sort made when metal strikes metal. Harry Fox had been facing her and jamming a shovel in the ground when she first glimpsed him. Now he had his back to her and had tossed the shovel on the ground. As she watched, he bent over and then stood, or at least tried to, grunting and cursing colorfully enough to make one side of her lip turn up. He was heaving at something, but she couldn't see what it was. Tom tapped her leg, so she turned to give an update. "He's pulling—oh my."

Tom came up beside her. "Is that a stone manhole cover?"

Harry Fox stood with his back to them, looking down into a dark hole as he held the edge of a stone slab with both hands. The slab appeared to be anchored to the ground in some way. As they watched, he lifted the slab until it balanced upright and stayed there. A moment later Harry removed a flashlight from his pack and aimed it at the dark spot on the ground. He paused, angling the light this way and that. Lauren reached out and pulled Tom back with her, dipping down so their heads were almost entirely hidden. Good thing they did. Harry Fox turned around in a hurry, looking directly where they'd been standing. Her hand latched onto Tom's arm as they both kept still. Harry seemed to narrow his gaze, lingering on the same spot, as if staring at them. She held her breath.

He turned back to the hole. Lauren blew air between her lips and let go of Tom. They watched Harry descend into the ground until he disappeared. The stone lid remained propped up and open.

This time Lauren led the charge without asking first. "Let's find out what this is." She took off at a jog. Tom followed behind, their footsteps silent on the lush grass as they went down the sloping ground only to quickly rise again, on a direct line for the vertical stone. The hole in the ground came into view as they drew closer, Lauren stopping several feet back and motioning for Tom to do the same.

Tom tapped her arm and made a circling motion with one hand, pointing to the rear of the raised stone. *I'll go around.* Lauren nodded and let him take a wide path until he stood behind the open stone. Only once Tom was in place did she approach the opening. This time she crouched low to stay out of sight, moving until she took one final step and peered down into the hole.

Roughly cut stone steps descended into darkness. Her shadow fell to one side, not down the steps, so it wouldn't give her away. She squinted but didn't see any sign of Harry. Not that she would have noticed him. Not with what lay at the bottom of the stairs.

Two full skeletons sitting against a side wall. The off-white bones of what appeared to be two adults, possibly in the same position as when they'd died. The room below was perhaps ten feet across and deep enough that she couldn't see the far end. Stones had been placed to make walls, though the floor was dirt. One room, or more than that?

Lauren looked up and motioned to Tom. *I'm going down.* His head shook vigorously and he lifted a palm toward her. *Wait.*

Her turn to shake her head. No way was she waiting when the answers could be right under her feet. Harry Fox might have taken another way out and slipped past them again.

She lay down on the ground in front of the first step to get her face as close to ground level as possible before she slid forward and angled her head into the room. Drops of moisture glistened on the stone stairs ahead, and the outline of wet footprints ran across the floor from the bottom step and out of sight. Harry Fox was down there. Absent another exit, they had him trapped.

Lauren crept over to Tom and put her mouth by his ear to describe what she'd seen and her concern about a second exit. "I say we go down there," she whispered. "Tell him we are government officials."

"He could have a gun."

"How would he get a gun into Ireland?" Tom had no good answer for that. "Besides, I'm a woman. Nobody shoots a woman." Tom didn't look so sure, so she ignored him. "Then we're agreed," Lauren said. "You go first."

His eyes went wide. "I'll go first," Lauren said. "Back me up on whatever I say."

Tom's face betrayed his misgivings about her plan, so she turned and made for the stairs before he could object. She stood at the top, pushed the thought of those two skeletons from her mind.

Lauren took a deep breath and shouted. "Look at this!" Tom jumped at the strength of her words. "There's an opening here," she said.

She marched down the stairs without hesitation. Harry Fox and anyone within a quarter mile would know they were here. "Skeletons," Lauren said to Tom as he followed her. "Be careful. Don't touch anything."

Tom spoke up. "What is this place?" he asked.

Good. Harry knew at least two people were here. Lauren went down the stairs at full speed. The darkness underground turned everything ahead of her to shadows. She stopped at the bottom of the stairs and narrowed her eyes at the outline of the man standing ahead of her. Harry Fox. "What are you doing down here?" she thundered. Her words bounced off the walls. "This is restricted government land."

"I'm a tourist." The man's voice had an unmistakable New York accent. "I just found this place and wanted to see what's down here. Am I not allowed?"

Lauren plowed on. "You didn't just stumble onto this place. You dug a hole in the park. Why are you down here with two skeletons?"

Harry stood no more than twenty feet ahead of her as Tom moved to stand beside her. Both looked at Harry, who held a rectangular object in his hands. He did not appear to be armed. "I'm sorry," he said. "I found an entrance to this place just now. What is it?"

Lauren looked past Harry to the rear chamber wall. A stone pedestal stood there, reaching about to waist height. A pedestal with nothing on top of it. "What are you holding?" Lauren asked. "Where did you get it?"

Harry wasn't fazed. "On the ground," he said as he looked at Tom. "I was just checking to see if it's damaged."

Tom jumped in. "You should not be down here."

Harry shrugged and offered an easy grin. "I thought it was part of the site. The door had a ring on it. I opened it."

"This door is not to be opened by an American tourist," Tom said.

Harry's easy grin froze. *He knows I'm American.* Tom didn't seem to notice. Lauren did.

"I'm sorry," Harry said quietly. "I didn't mean to cause trouble. Here." He offered the tablet he was holding to Tom. "This tablet caught my attention." His eyes never left Tom's face. "I wanted to see what was written on it."

Tom practically leapt forward to take the proffered tablet. The hair on Lauren's neck went up as he did. She caught a glimpse of an object carved into the tablet. Something was wrong here.

Too late. Tom took a step toward Harry and then it happened. One instant, Tom's fingers grazed the stone tablet. The next, Harry darted in close and slammed the edge of the tablet into Tom's stomach. Tom doubled over and Harry crouched, sweeping his leg out to send Tom sprawling before Harry shot up to grab Lauren's arm, pulling her toward him before throwing her back toward the empty pedestal. Not hard enough to injure, but with sufficient force that she had to brace herself to keep from hitting the rear wall. She bounced off and turned to find him halfway up the stairs. "Stop!" she shouted.

Lauren only made it to the foot of the stairs before the stone lid slammed down from above and darkness surrounded them.

They were trapped, and Harry Fox was again on the loose. With a tablet that could hold the key to the entire mystery.

Chapter 7

Hill of Tara, County Meath

Shouting came from the ground. Spirits from the underworld screaming to the heavens.

Or that's what pagans from the time of ancient Brittania might have thought if they'd heard the ruckus coming from the underground chamber near the Fal Stone. Harry Fox stood on top of the stone cover, fighting the feeling this was a mistake. He should run. Run fast, and run far. That's exactly what he'd done after slamming the lid on these impostors. Then his gut jumped in and quashed the idea.

They knew he was American. That's what tipped him off. Or was the man's statement a lucky guess, Harry's accent giving the clue? Possibly, but the guy seemed so *sure*. How would a Public Works employee who just happened upon Harry know he was American with such certainty? Only one answer made sense.

These two were not Public Works employees. Who were they? He knelt and put an ear close to a corner of the lid. Their voices came through. He grinned. Score one for the good guys.

"Can you lift it?" The woman's voice reached his ear first. Irish accent, if he had to guess, and she did not sound happy.

The stone beneath his feet shuddered. "It's stuck," the man said. Irish accent as well, and the guy was strong. Harry went up a few inches as the guy pushed on the stone lid. "Come over here and help me," the man said. "This is heavy."

Harry moved up and down a few more times, his weight enough to keep the lid closed.

"How are we going to get out of here?" the woman asked. "Hang on. I have my phone."

"Do you have service?" the man asked. "I don't have any signal down here."

"Turn your light on so I can see," the woman said. "Maybe I can get a bar at the top of the stairs."

The sound of footsteps as she climbed the steps. "I have a signal." Her voice was louder now, the only thing between her and Harry the stone beneath his feet. "I'm calling for backup."

Harry looked up. The two druids were nowhere to be seen. He had the park to himself. Well, the above-ground part, at least. He could spare another minute.

"It's me, Lauren. We found Harry Fox."

I knew it. They knew him. His chest tightened. What else did they know?

"He found a hidden chamber at the Hill of Tara. We followed and now we're stuck in the chamber." A beat passed. "We need you to come get us out of here. Now." Another beat. "I have no idea where he went. He has a tablet he took from this chamber and we need to recover it."

The woman explained how to find the chamber cover as Harry's eyebrows rose. These people weren't with the government. But they knew about the trail to the Four Treasures of the Tuatha Dé Danann.

Most importantly, these people believed it was real. This relic hunt had now become a race, and Harry Fox was in the lead.

Another bump from below as they tried to lift it again. "Give it a rest," the man said. "They'll be here in twenty minutes."

"He could be anywhere by then."

"As long as he keeps that rental vehicle, we can find him," the man said. "He can't turn the GPS off."

Thanks for the tip. Harry stood and moved as quietly as possible off the lid so as not to alert them, then took off running, holding the tablet tightly until he made it to his car and had the door open. He fired the engine, slammed it into first gear, and took off in a spray of gravel as a map of Ireland filled his head. Dublin lay perhaps forty minutes southeast of here. Plenty of places to return his rental car and figure out another way to get around. How had they tracked this specific rental car? What to do next? Talking to someone who had run this sort of race before made sense. Good thing for Harry he knew just the man.

Ringing sounded as he dialed a number and put his phone on speaker. The man answered at once. "Everything okay?"

"What makes you think it's not?" Harry asked.

Fred Fox chuckled. "I'll try again. Have you solved the mystery yet?"

"Work proceeds apace," Harry said. "I need your advice. I've had"—he hesitated here—"an interesting development."

Any levity in Fred's voice disappeared. "I'm listening."

Trees whizzed past as Harry recapped the events around the Fal Stone, including an abbreviated version of his trek through the castle and how a windowsill carving had revealed an identical image in the nearby hills that marked a hidden cavern. "I found another tablet inside."

"Is there writing on it?" Fred asked.

Harry glanced at the tablet. "Yes. A carving and Latin text."

He eased off the gas and settled on a speed within shouting distance of the limit. One eye stayed on the road. The other went to his new prize. "It's the same size as the tablet I found in the cave. Same shape and color too. Which isn't even the best part."

"I'm waiting."

Jeez, Dad. It's my first relic chase. Let me enjoy it. "The upper half is filled with Latin letters. The bottom half contains an image of a spear. A very familiar one, if I'm any judge."

"It's the same spear you found on the cave tablet."

"How did you know?"

"This isn't my first treasure hunt."

It took Harry a second to get going again. "It's the exact same image."

"Which suggests what?"

"The spear is the next treasure I'll find."

"Unless this all goes sideways," Fred said. "But yes. My thought is this new tablet points to the spear. Does the message on the tablet support the idea?"

"You tell me." He held the tablet in front of him to better read. "It's one sentence." Harry read the Latin in English. "*Follow the warrior's path to Aed, who protects our treasure in his domain.*"

Fred kept silent. Harry let it carry on. "Any thoughts?" Fred finally asked.

"I haven't had a chance to research anything yet," Harry said. "The name *Aed* rings a bell. Can't say from where off the top of my head."

"Aed is the god of the underworld in Irish myth."

"And you know that how?"

"My son is chasing a relic tied to Irish mythology. I read up on it."

"I can handle this myself."

Fred sighed. "Harry, what have I told you about asking for help?"

"Only fools think they can do everything alone." It was Harry's turn to let out a sigh. "Seeing farther and standing on giants' shoulders, that sort of thing. I get it."

"Your quotation could use a tweak," Fred said. "But that's the gist of it. Don't be afraid to ask for help. But following this message should not be at the top of your list."

"What should?"

"Getting rid of that rental car."

Fred had a point. "I'm working on that now."

"You have a plan?"

"Get a new car near Dublin."

"How will you do that without showing identification?"

"I can't."

"Correct, so you'll need to move fast." A pause. "You could ask for help from one of Vincent Morello's contacts. Which I do not suggest."

"Why not?"

"Prove you can handle yourself in the field first. Then ask for favors."

Another fair point. "Then it sounds like I need to move quickly. Stay ahead of them."

"Exactly," Fred said. "Right after you ask me to dig into this question about Aed while you get a new car."

"I'll return this and then get a different car from a different rental place."

"That will buy you a bit of time," Fred said. "I'll look into the Aed angle. Which isn't the only part that tells us more about this chase."

"What else jumps out at you?" Harry asked.

"The message talks about *our treasure*. Which lends credence to the idea this is about an entire people and their ideas, their faith. It's not merely one treasure. We're dealing with a greater idea."

"That makes sense."

"It should also make you worried. These people following you will not let their treasure be taken without a fight."

Harry ignored the tightening in his stomach. "Thanks for the pep talk."

"Better to over-prepare than the alternative," Fred said. "Trust me on that one."

"I'll call you once I have a new car," Harry said. "And I'll be ready for a class on Aed."

"Give the tablet a thorough inspection after you have the new car. Consider what else it may have to say."

Fred clicked off with that vague advice. Harry found his gaze drawn toward the stone tablet as the people started to outnumber cows beyond his window and the countryside crept toward urban. He was drawn to the image, not the words. Did the spear contain a larger meaning? Perhaps that this stage of his quest required a battle, or the need to prepare for one? Those thoughts filled his head until he realized he was halfway into Dublin and had probably passed a half-dozen car rental options.

He pulled off and found a branch of the car rental agency he had used, motoring to it and dropping off his vehicle. No, he did not need anything else. No, he did not want to leave a review. He pushed his way through the door and back into the minimal Dublin sun, walking several blocks at random before looking for another rental agency on his phone. The tablet seemed to weigh more than it should in his pack as he walked a half-mile to the new rental location. Speed mattered here. Stay ahead of the pursuit. A bored-looking desk attendant offered Harry his choice of cars on the lot and Harry soon found himself behind the wheel of a sports car whose name he couldn't pronounce and didn't care to learn. He knew all he needed to know when the key turned and the engine roared. This car could move.

He managed to get out of the lot without laying any tire. The clutch was long, the gears finely tuned, and he burned a gallon of gas ripping down a few city streets until he got a feel for the sporting machine. He pulled into a gas station by an exit for the highway, cut the engine, and opened his pack. A feeling he couldn't quite put a name to had taken root on the drive into Dublin. His father had told him to give the tablet a closer look. Why would he say that? Experience.

He inspected the carved words. Ran his finger around and over them. Nothing stood out. Next came the carving. A familiar spear, not much more than a triangular blade on the end of a stick decorated with what looked like rope or fabric. Again, nothing jumped out. "It's not the writing or the spear," he said to himself. "What about the stone itself?"

He hefted the tablet. About the size of a paperback novel, it was heavy, but not overly so. Under closer inspection the stone itself revealed nothing. Dark gray, not exactly uniform in color, and rough to the touch. He twisted it. He flipped it around. He rapped a knuckle on the front. "It's a stone."

Harry blew air between his lips, the tablet held in both hands, and he shook his head. *This is all getting to me.* Following an ancient trail with a mysterious duo right behind him. Exactly what he'd always wanted, and now he couldn't keep focused. He gritted his teeth. "Think. Dad always said the answers are there; you just have to look in the right place." So why couldn't he figure out what the heck this tablet meant? What was the warrior's path to Aed, and how did he follow it? He had no clue.

In frustration he slapped the bottom of the tablet with one hand. Smacked it hard. So hard his hand stung when he pulled it back and shook it.

A piece of stone fell in his lap.

Harry stopped shaking his hand. He went still, his eyes locked onto the hunk of rock in his lap. A perfect rectangle of rock about the size of a pack of gum sat on his lap. Where had it come from? He angled the tablet to look at the bottom. "No way."

The tablet had a hidden compartment in the bottom. A compartment that was not empty.

Harry removed a rolled scrap of parchment from the small chamber. "This is papyrus." A correct material for the time period when Romans had come to Brittania. The ancient Irish would have used this. "But they hardly ever wrote anything down," Harry said. He set the tablet down, held the papyrus with a gentle touch, and unrolled it.

Latin writing.

"*The Romans come. Do not break the tie between Aed and his father.*"

Harry looked up before reading the rest of the message. "This tells us what to do next."

Chapter 8

Hill of Tara, County Meath

"Help me try again."

Lauren activated the flashlight app on her phone to light the subterranean chamber. "We can't sit here while he gets away."

Tom O'Malley remained seated on the bottom step. "Help will be here soon."

"Harry Fox is getting away."

"I hate to have to tell you this, Lauren. He's already gone." Tom gestured at the stone slab above them. "We can't do anything until that thing is moved. So have a seat. We won't be here much longer."

She crossed her arms. "No. We're getting it open. Right now."

Lauren grabbed Tom's arm and tried to rip him from the step. "Get up." She succeeded only in knocking him onto the ground. "Get on your feet. Help me."

Tom grumbled something she thankfully didn't catch. "Save your energy. All you'll do is hurt yourself."

She crossed her arms. "You don't think I can lift it?"

"No." Tom slowly got to his feet, standing in front of her and looking down right into her eyes. "I do not. Do you know why? Because I can't, and I'm stronger than you."

"We can lift it if we both push together."

Tom looked up at the dark stone. "Maybe. But why bother? We'll be out of here in"—he checked his watch—"twenty minutes. Maybe less."

"Which gives him a great head start."

"Lauren, he's in the wind for now." Tom patted her on the shoulder. "Only for now. You can track his car."

She wasn't having it. "Only if he keeps using that car. What if he realizes that's how I tracked him? He's not dim. He made it here." She waved at the chamber in which they were entombed. "He made more progress in a few days than we did in centuries. The man's good. He'll figure out how we found him soon. Once that happens, we're lost." She grabbed Tom's arm and dragged him up the stairs with her. "We can move this if we lift together. Come on."

Lauren put her shoulder against the stone cover where it met the top stair and heaved. She did it again, making a noise of exertion that far exceeded her efforts while glaring at Tom below her.

"Fine," he said. He climbed the steps and put a shoulder on the cover. "Waste of time," he said.

"What's that?" she asked.

"Nothing. Ready? Push!"

Lauren shoved with everything she had as Tom did the same. The slab held firm.

"It's no use." Heavy breaths came and went as Tom moved to sit on the steps. "You have to pull the handle from outside to lift it."

"I felt it move," she said. "Come on. One more try. Then I'll leave you alone."

Tom looked at her askance. "Fine. If only to keep you quiet."

Shoulders returned to the stone. They counted down, and this time when they pushed Lauren really did feel movement. The rock shifted up. Neither spoke, both of them pushing up to keep the stone moving until they could take a step up and get more leverage to push it higher. The outside world appeared and they heaved until they both were on the top step.

"You go first," Tom said through clenched teeth. "Slide out and grab the ring."

She wriggled out the opening, stood up on the grass and grabbed hold of the iron ring to pull the stone cover up. "Get out," she shouted. "This is heavy."

Tom shoved the lid up as she pushed and the stone flipped on its hinges. Lauren only noticed anything wrong when Tom loosed an anguished cry. She looked down to find Tom sprawled out on the top step, clutching his ankle.

"What happened?" Lauren left the cover upright and darted around to where Tom was lying on the grass. "Are you okay?"

"Twisted my ankle. Caught it on the lip as I tried to step out. It's my fault."

"Let me see it." She knelt beside him, gently pushing one of his hands away to probe at the injured ankle.

"Ouch!" Tom jerked his ankle away. "Don't touch it." He got onto one foot.

"How bad is it?" she asked as she helped him up.

He leaned a fraction of his weight on it. The shouted curses were answer enough. "I can't walk on it," Tom said. "I can't believe I did that."

"I'm so sorry," she said. "You were right. We should have waited for help."

"I'm the one who tripped over his own feet." Tom pointed toward the car park. "Help me get over there." He immediately stopped. "Wait." Tom looked back into the chamber. "I don't think there's anything else to find down there, but go take a look before anyone else shows up."

She left him standing on one leg and went back underground, casting a wary eye at the cover as she descended. A brief search found Tom had been correct. "There's nothing else," she said as she came back up the stairs. "An empty pedestal and empty walls. Harry Fox took the only thing that mattered in that room."

"The tablet," Tom said. "Which you will recover. After you pay him back for my ankle. I'll send some real muscle with you to sort him out properly."

"No."

Both were equally surprised by her response. "You have a better idea?" Tom asked.

"We don't need muscle. He's used to that. Harry Fox understands how to fight. He's smart. He beat us here and then escaped. We had him, Tom, and he got past us." She tapped the side of her head. "We need to be smarter."

Tom wasn't having it. "You have no idea where he went. How can you beat him without help?"

"I think I know where to find him. The tablet he took—I saw what was on it."

Tom was suddenly all ears. "What did you see?"

"A spear."

The air went out of Tom. "A spear. You saw a spear, and you think you know where to find him."

"I do, and I'll tell you why. The first tablet led him here, to the Fal Stone, which is one of the Four Treasures, and it stands near a Celtic cross. What if that's the tie? A Celtic cross and a link to the Four Treasures."

"Sounds crazy." Tom waved a dismissive hand, then lowered it, looking at her curiously. "But go on."

"The spear could be next in line." Her words quickened as she spoke. "The tablet may point to a location marked by a spear and a Celtic cross."

"And you know such a place?"

"We both do." A breeze rustled the grass at her feet. "Kealkill Circle."

"There's no—hang on, there is. There's a spear at the circle. And a cross." Tom rubbed his forehead. "You can't truly believe this."

"I do," Lauren said. "The spear stone."

Kealkill Circle stood several hours away. A well-known historical site, it was a circle of a half-dozen stones dating to before the Common Era, which put it squarely in the time of ancient Brittania. One stone stood out from the others. The only stone with any decoration at all. A carving of a spear. Which, if memory served, looked quite a bit like the one she'd glimpsed on the tablet.

"It even looks like the spear on the tablet," she said, thinking aloud.

"You don't know that," Tom said. "You saw it for an instant."

True, but she wasn't admitting anything. "I'm certain." She wasn't. "I have a better plan than sending more people after him," Lauren continued.

"Not just people," Tom said. "One person. Maurice Keane."

Lauren shook her head. "Maurice has too much of a temper."

Maurice Keane and Tom O'Connor had been friends since they were young boys playing on the streets of Dublin. Maurice never talked much. He kept to himself, listened instead of talked, and, for such a big man, did an impressive job of fading into the background. At least until his temper got up. A switch flipped when Maurice got angry. Lauren had never been on the receiving end when Maurice, well, when *Maurice* happened.

"That's an especially bad idea."

"Good thing for me you're not in charge."

"Listen to me. I can do this alone. I can find Harry Fox."

"Based on a glimpse of a tablet? You have no evidence." Tom grimaced as he shifted his weight. "Not to mention I can't go with yo—"

"I don't need you."

Tom raised a hand. "I have no doubts you can handle yourself."

"Then why send Maurice Keane?"

Tom considered. "Because Harry Fox is capable. He could also be dangerous. I've known Maurice my entire life. I trust him to take my place, which includes looking out for you."

"Maurice is a human wrecking ball."

Tom didn't argue. "I can get to Kealkill Circle quickly," she said. "I'll find Harry Fox, learn what he knows, and get ahead of him in this race."

"How will you get close to him? He'll recognize you straight off."

"He didn't see my face. Think about it." She moved to stand behind Tom. "You were between us the entire time. It was dark. I never said anything in my normal voice. I was shouting the whole time, trying to sound official. He won't recognize me."

"You're willing to bet your life on it?"

"Harry Fox doesn't want to hurt us."

"Could have fooled me. Slamming that big stone on top of us and all."

"He was trying to get away." She was reaching and she knew it. She didn't care. "I can gain his trust. Get him to tell me what he knows."

"He's in a foreign land. He has no friends here."

"None we know of."

She ignored him. "I can convince him I'm a local when our paths cross. Give me a day. Two at the most. We'll know if he has the same rental car by then. If I can't find him, or if I can't get what I need, we do it your way."

"You'll go to Kealkill, see if you can find this guy, somehow get the tablet or learn what's on it, and then get ahead of him. That's your plan?"

Lauren nodded. "That's the long and short of it."

Tom chuckled. "Full marks for confidence, I'll give you that." The chuckle turned to a grimace of pain. "Best get moving. I'll keep an eye on this chamber while you're running around."

"Is this the part where you tell me you'll be waiting after I find nothing at Kealkill?"

"I hope your scheme works, but you know that hope is a terrible plan, which is why we make backup plans. That's Maurice." He gently pushed her away. "Go and prove me wrong about needing Maurice."

She ran. Down the hill past the Fal Stone and the small knots of tourists who had appeared. Her last glimpse of Tom before she got in her car and raced off was of him sitting on the cavern entrance, one hand raised in farewell.

As Lauren gained the open road, she pushed the gas pedal a little harder. *I'm coming for you, Harry Fox.*

Chapter 9

Kealkill Circle, County Cork

A *Welcome* sign against the vibrant green landscape announced the village of Kealkill. Lauren passed short hedgerows fronting buildings painted in pastel colors, a petrol station and a single pub. She peered at every person outside each door and vehicle, which is to say she studied a half-dozen people before she was through the town and back into open countryside. Lauren Brosnan had grown up in Ireland and been to many villages like this, but she was still surprised at how small it was. She grinned. "You can't hide here, Harry Fox."

She pulled off at the first dirt road, turning around and going back through town again. People noticed an outsider. If a man who looked like Harry Fox had arrived it would raise a few eyebrows. Unfortunately, the same could be said for her. People in places like this didn't often talk to strangers. They welcomed them, smiled at them, and hoped they spent a few pounds, but they didn't open up to them. Even fellow Irish could receive the cold shoulder if they got too personal. Lauren spotted a group of people just outside of the local market. She pulled off and parked her vehicle. Time to see how Irish she could be.

She shook her hair from its braid, let her Irish curls loose, and put on a pair of glasses she found buried in her purse. Changing her appearance even a little might fool Harry Fox. He'd only had a glimpse of her near the Fal Stone.

She stretched her back as she got out; the four hours spent racing across Ireland had taken their toll. The trio of women standing in the late afternoon sunlight outside the market entrance gave her only a glance as she approached.

"*Dia duit,*" Lauren said, offering them a greeting in Irish. The three women looked her up and down before the youngest among them responded with caution.

"Hello," she replied in the same language.

"I'm in town from Dublin," Lauren said. "Haven't been in Kealkill before and I'm a bit lost. Would you be able to point me to the Circle?"

The common term for the stone circle was clearly understood. "Take that road south and it will be on the right," the same girl said. "There are signs. You cannot miss it."

"Thank you." Lauren put on a friendly smile. "I'm hoping to meet a friend there. I thought he would be here in town, but I can't seem to find him."

She let the silence linger. The two older women didn't seem interested in responding. The girl, however, did answer. "What's he look like?" she asked, then listened as Lauren described Harry. "I haven't seen him," the girl said. "Have you lot?" she asked her two companions. Both made noncommittal noises.

Lauren's face stayed positive. "I'm sure he'll turn up," she said.

The girl perked up. "Wait. I did see someone when I left my house to come here."

Hope sprang to life in Lauren's chest. "Did it look like him? I'm worried his phone is broken and he can't call me."

"Not sure what he looked like," the girl said. "He was too far away. But he was definitely headed toward the Circle."

Lauren thanked her and turned back to her car. Her mind and eyes were on the road ahead as she drove, the quaint Irish town forgotten until she came around a curve in the road and nearly rear-ended a car parked on the verge. She veered around it and stopped beside the low metal gate that protected a dirt path leading up a slight rise.

A sign no bigger than a shoebox told everyone what waited ahead. *Kealkill Stone Circle.*

Lauren turned her car off, twisted round in her seat and studied the vehicle parked behind her. Not the same one Harry Fox had escaped in. If this was his, he had changed cars. The lone man standing at the top of the gently sloping rise above her? That man hadn't changed one bit. "Harry Fox," she said to herself. "Found you."

The stone circle was up a dirt road that consisted of two tire tracks through knee-high grass. Lauren reached into her purse, retrieved her cell phone and pulled up Tom O'Malley's number. She looked down at the bright phone screen but did not touch it. She should call Tom right now. Report that their target had been located. Her hunch had been correct— *Well done, Lauren*—and now it was time to relinquish control over what came next.

Which meant Tom and Maurice would arrive to bulldoze the opposition. Harry would be no match for the two of them. Yet Harry was still on the hunt and might already know more than they realized. Tom would come right after Harry, because Harry Fox was the first true lead in their lifetimes. Tom wouldn't be able to help himself. A chance to be the one who uncovered the truth that began at the Fal Stone? Heaven help anyone who stood in his way.

Lauren tapped one finger on her leg, over and over. She couldn't escape the idea she had become what Tom despised. A person who stood against him and in the way of his mission. Not due to her wanting him to fail, though—Lauren wanted the same outcome as

Tom: to find the treasures and prove the current Irish government was not the rightful leader of Ireland. Their difference lay in the approach. Tom strong-arming Harry in the middle of his search would never get Harry to tell them everything he knew. Brute force wasn't the answer here. This called for a lighter touch.

Lauren tapped out her message to Tom. *En route to Kealkill. Will report back.* The phone went into her pocket and she opened the car door, getting out and taking the first steps on a new mission. One in which Lauren made the calls. At least for now.

Rocks crunched underfoot as she meandered up the dirt road toward where Harry stood on the small hill. Five stones of varying sizes surrounded him. None reached higher than his chest. She glanced at him as she walked, smiling and giving a half-wave as she approached. He did not return either until she reached the end of the path and faced him. She reached into her pocket. He tensed. She pulled out her phone, casually turned her back to him, and began taking pictures.

Pictures of Harry Fox. She had reversed the camera on her phone so it displayed the view over her shoulder. A clear image of the man behind her watching as she captured images of her quarry. Low-hanging thin white clouds eased across the sky as she watched Harry watching her. He hadn't taken his eyes off her since she'd turned her camera on him. He wasn't moving. Just watching.

She turned slowly around. "Hello," she said. He didn't react. "Lovely day for a visit."

"It is."

She waited. It seemed Harry Fox didn't fall for the temptation to fill silence with words. "It's difficult to believe this circle has lasted for so long." She walked toward the nearest stone and stood before it, not quite touching the weathered rock. "An enduring monument, but to what?" A puff of wind blew hair across her face. She did not pull it back. "I love the mystery."

"Perhaps it's a marker," Harry said. "A message from the past."

"A message?" Lauren lifted a shoulder. "Don't those often involve words? Or a drawing, at least?"

"Not always." He turned away from her and the stones, his gaze now on a Celtic cross adjacent to the circle. A cross identical to the cross by the Fal Stone.

It seemed he was serious about being quiet. "I haven't seen you here before," Lauren said. She marched right over to him and stuck a hand out. "My name's Lauren."

"Nice to meet you, Lauren." Harry didn't offer his name, though he did take her hand. Calluses scratched her palm when they shook. "I've never been here before."

He wasn't as tall as she remembered. A few inches above her and no more. Fit, and she put him at under thirty. He could use a shave. "It's an out-of-the-way place," Lauren said. "But worth the visit." She turned away as though to admire the nearest stone. "For me, at least." Harry made something close to a grunt. Of agreement or disinterest, hard to say. She sensed his interest waning. "You're not from Ireland." A statement, not a question. Which could have the same effect."

"I'm not."

"What brings you to this quiet part of the country?"

"These stones."

Not much for small talk. Not yet. Lauren ran a hand through her hair, adjusted her glasses, and inched closer to him. "If you came all this way for a message, you may be disappointed." She smiled and flicked her hair again. Harry Fox didn't even look. So much for the coquettish angle. *Not your type? Fine. Try this one on.* "Would you mind taking a picture for me?" she asked. "I need proof of a measurement and I can't hold the pen myself."

That got his ear. "Hold a pen? Why are you measuring with a pen?"

"I forgot my tape measure," she shot back. "I can't finish a dissertation with faulty measurements now, can I?" She lightly touched his arm and pulled him toward the nearest rock. "It won't take a second."

A pen came out of her pocket and she held it by a random part of the stone. "Come on," she said. "Two shots." He looked at her with his head at an angle as she handed over her phone, then took the shots. "Thanks," she said as she took her phone back. "I'm a stickler for accuracy."

This time he didn't look away when she turned. Any second now.

"Did you say dissertation?"

"I did," she said without looking at him.

Harry Fox may have found the hidden chamber in Dunmore Cave and a cavern by the Fal Stone. That didn't mean he knew anything about Kealkill Circle. "About this stone circle?" he asked.

She pretended to scrutinize her photograph and ignored the question. "I need one more shot. The angle isn't great." He didn't resist when she handed her phone over and made him take one more image. "That works," she said after getting her phone back. "You aren't a bad photographer for a Yank."

"What makes you think I'm American?"

"Easy to recognize a New York accent."

A flicker of a smile crossed his face. "Fair enough." The flicker vanished. "What do you know about this stone circle?"

She made a face as though the question surprised her. "Quite a lot." Lauren waved a hand. "You want to know about the stones. Is that why you're here." Harry shook his head. "Then why come all the way out here?" she asked.

"Treasure."

He grinned. A nice grin, one meant to disarm. "Oh." She let her shoulders slump. "One of those."

"What's that mean?" he asked. Too quickly.

"You're not the first treasure hunter I've seen here." She put her hands on her hips. "You think you'll find gold or jewels? Sorry to tell you. There's none to be found."

"I'm not... I'm not a relic—I mean a treasure hunter."

"Treasure hunter?"

"I'm here on a search, yes." Another pause. "For a contest."

Her eyebrows came together. "A treasure-hunting contest?"

"Yes," and here his words finally gained steam. "There's a prize. It's held by a group I belong to. One of the members put together clues everyone has to follow, and the first person to find a treasure at the end of the path wins."

"What do you win?"

He made an exaggerated gesture of putting his finger to his lips. "It's a secret. Nobody knows what it is until the game is over."

"So you came here from New York as part of a game?"

"More of a hobby."

She had put her bait in the water by posing as a researcher. Harry had taken it. Lauren moved to set the hook. "These stones are a clue in your game?" she asked. Harry nodded. "Would you like help? I've studied most of the stone circles in Ireland." A lie, but she'd make up what she didn't know.

"You'd help me?"

Lauren shrugged. "It sounds interesting."

"It is. But I need to show you something first." He dropped his voice. "You can't tell anyone. Deal?"

Her heart quickened. "Deal. What is the big secret?"

"It's more of a small secret." Harry went to a small pack sitting on the ground nearby and removed a rectangular object. Roughly the size of a paperback novel, brownish-gray in color. A hunk of stone that Lauren had seen before. "This is it," Harry said. "There's writing on one side of it." He turned it around to display said writing. "It's in—"

"—Latin." It took a force of will not to rip the tablet from his hands. "May I hold it?"

Harry hesitated, then shrugged. "Sure. It's part of the game. Makes it seem real."

She handled the stone clue with unusual care. "Incredible," Lauren said. "They made it look real."

"I'll translate what's on it," Harry replied, but Lauren beat him to it.

"*Follow the warrior's path to Aed, who protects our treasure in his domain.*" She finished reading and looked up to find Harry's jaw had dropped. "Is that your translation too?" she asked.

It took a beat for his mouth to work. "You read Latin?"

"I'd ask you the same."

He blinked. "Yes, I can read it. Learned in school." A laugh that wasn't quite a laugh. "Never thought it would be useful."

"Are you familiar with the god Aed?" Lauren asked. Harry rattled off a fairly accurate summary. "That would be a yes," Lauren said. "God of the underworld in our mythology. Though what Aed has to do with this image on your tablet is beyond me." She angled the tablet to catch the sunlight. "Is this a spear?"

"What makes you say that?"

Clever. Harry wanted her to keep sharing information, and she would. For now. "It looks like a spear," she said flatly. "What's it look like to you?"

"A spear."

"Which means what?"

Harry shrugged. "I'm not sure."

"How did you know to bring this tablet to Kealkill Circle?" she asked.

The unscripted broadside put him on his back foot. "We were told to start here," he said after only a moment's hesitation. "This is the first location."

"Does the spear image have any tie to this location?" she asked.

Harry grinned. "I hope you know the answer to that."

"I do." She winked. "I can't help you win this race too quickly, can I?" Lauren pointed to the largest standing stone in the circle. "It ties to that stone. The spear stone. An image of a spear is carved into it. Hard to see now, though it's there if you look from the proper angle. Do you see it?" Harry said he did. "Then I believe that's where we should focus."

"Does the Celtic cross have anything to do with a spear or Aed?" Harry asked.

Lauren looked to the nearby cross, one nearly identical to the cross by the Fal Stone and the connection that had given this location away. "Not that I'm aware of," she said honestly. "The spear stone connection is fairly obvious. Did you expect the contest to be more challenging? Anyone with a smartphone could discover that a stone at this circle has a spear image."

Harry seemed to have an answer for everything. "We're not supposed to use technology," he said without hesitating. "The internet is off limits. Research should mean a trip to the library."

"Or consulting with an expert like me."

"That's allowed."

The gentle breeze, the landscape painted by sunlight, Harry Fox. All of them faded as she held the tablet, staring at it as though by sheer force alone she could discern the answer to its riddle. Aed? She knew of him, knew his history, but he had no specific association with this area.

"This could be entirely off base."

Harry's voice made her look up. "What could?"

"I found several references to a pagan holiday in my research," he said. "Midsummer."

That was more familiar ground. "The Briton festival celebrating the summer solstice," she said. "What about it?"

"Yes," he said. "It's Brittonic." Did he look at her a shade more closely? "It's also celebrated by many other cultures."

"Who appropriated it." Her sharp retort came without thinking. "Which is how you should view it for the purposes of your treasure hunt," she said quickly. "Do you know the history of Midsummer?"

"Not as well as you."

"The origins date back to before the Common Era," she said. "You'll know stone circles are central to observing the holiday."

"As in having the sunrise on the summer solstice aligned to the layout of Stonehenge?"

"To cite the most famous example. Other circles have similar functions." She adjusted her glasses and looked directly at him. "Most people don't realize Midsummer is still celebrated today by most Christians around the world."

"Saint John's Day."

"That's right." She hadn't seen that coming. "Christianity uses the same day for their holiday as the one Romans used for their Midsummer festivities. June twenty-fourth. I should have guessed you'd know that."

"The Romans honored their goddess Fors Fortuna," Harry said correctly. "The goddess of luck."

"Lucky is what early civilizations thought themselves when the days lengthened and the temperatures rose. The sun brought long days, and more importantly, food. Crops grew during the summer. Without those sunny days, they died."

"And where did the Romans get the idea of Fors Fortuna?" Harry asked. "I thought it was from the Greek goddess Tyche."

"In part," Lauren said. "Though Tyche was not the true source. That came from a different part of the world." She pointed at the dirt beneath their feet. "Right here."

"The ancient Irish," Harry said.

"Who celebrated Midsummer for the same reasons."

Harry rubbed the stubble on his chin. "We start with the ancient Irish, go to the Romans, and end with the Christians. I wonder why everyone was so interested in *borrowing* the others' beliefs?"

She stuck the tablet out. "If you don't know, then you should take this back right now and go on your way."

Harry lifted his eyebrows. "I don't know much of anything for sure. That doesn't mean I can't guess." Lauren waved at him to go on. "They all did it for the same reason most civilizations take on certain aspects of another. To help the old beliefs merge with the new."

"To destroy the old beliefs is what you mean." Lauren shook her head. "It's a story as old as time. What's the best way to conquer a people with minimal resistance? Make it seem as though they aren't being conquered at all. The Romans were masters of the tactic. Crush an army, but let the old gods and beliefs stay on. People were less likely to stop paying taxes and start fighting if they could still worship their gods."

"The Romans did it because it worked."

"They did it because they could," she fired back. "The mirage of independence is worse than subjugation. At least those in the latter camp know what's happening."

Harry rubbed his chin again. "Does this have anything to do with my treasure hunt?"

"You tell me." Now she tapped the tablet against her thigh. "I'm missing something." A thought crossed her mind as she turned the problem over. Hit Harry over the head with this tablet and be on her way. Do it when his back was turned and she'd put him down for sure. Long enough for her to get in her car and race away, at least, leaving Harry and his admittedly timely intrusion into her world as nothing but a story to tell around the table, a lesson in taking advantage of opportunity when it knocked on the door. A great tale, and a massive feather in her cap. Perhaps the first of many to come.

"I doubt that."

Harry's words pulled her back to the present. "What did you say?" she asked.

"I said I doubt that you'd miss anything." One corner of his mouth turned up and his eyes flashed mirth. "A scholar like you probably doesn't miss much."

And just like that, Harry Fox saved his skull. She couldn't hit him. Not now. The man had only met her a few minutes earlier and already he believed in her. Believed in her more than her Irish colleagues did. A guy like that deserved a chance. At least, for now. Maybe she'd whack him on the head next time. "It's this." She indicated the tablet. "What's written on this tablet doesn't tell the whole story. I can't say exactly why I feel this way. It seems, in a way, incomplete."

"One sentence isn't enough to reveal much."

"It's not," Lauren said. "There should be more. There *has* to be more." She tapped the engraving with a finger. "More than a simple spear."

"What else could it be?" Harry asked. "It is possible the stone here isn't Aed's spear?"

"Not that I see." She nodded to the stone with a spear cut into it. "That is Aed's spear. Of any spear in Ireland, that is Aed's. Your stone points here."

Lauren paused, and in that slight hesitation, Harry looked away. His gaze didn't turn. His face didn't move. Yet still she knew she had lost him. The unfocused eyes, the mouth hanging slightly open. Harry Fox stood in front of her, but his mind was far away. "What is it?" she asked.

It took him several seconds to respond. "You might be on to something."

"How so?"

He snapped his fingers. "Say that again. What you said about the stone and what it does."

What was he getting at? "That it points here?"

"You might be right."

"Might be? I'm certain it's correct. The standing stone is Aed's spear. The tablet leads here."

"Maybe. Maybe not. What if it's not the end? Could be this tablet only gets me partway to the true destination." He grabbed her gently by the shoulders and turned her to face the stone. "The tablet points here, to this stone with a spear on it. But where does the spear point?"

He adjusted her torso slightly. Enough that she no longer looked at the stone known as Aed's spear. Now she looked into the distance. "What am I supposed to see?" she asked.

"Where the spear points. I don't think it's a simple marker. I think it's a *directional* marker. Like an arrow."

"A marker pointing where?"

He put an arm up and pointed ahead. "Right there."

Lauren shielded her eyes against the sunlight. "I don't see anything." A small grouping of brown and white cows milled about in the distance, heads down in the grass as they ate. Small groups of leafy trees stood watch. Wildflowers bloomed a vibrant purple across the green grass. "There's nothing here but the countryside."

"What about that?" Harry motioned her over with his head and kept his arm steady. She frowned, decided to humor him, and then leaned down to sight along his outstretched arm as though it were a rifle. She spotted it at once, sitting several hundred yards distant. "A pile of stones?"

"Looks more like an old well to me. Any idea how long it's been here?"

"Perhaps a century. Perhaps twenty of them." She stood and stepped back into her personal space. "Why does a pile of stones matter?"

Harry's arm dropped, he picked up his pack and started walking. "Let's go find out."

She found herself hurrying to catch up without thinking. "Why does it matter?" she asked. "Even if it is a well, that has nothing to do with the Circle or Aed."

"Not on the surface." Harry kept up his pace as they went down a gently sloping hill before the ground leveled out. Tall grasses swayed as they passed. "But we're not dealing with anything on the surface here. We're dealing with Aed." He turned and winked at her. "God of the *underworld*."

He accelerated and didn't offer anything further as they covered the remaining short distance to the stones. Only once they stood beside it could Lauren see these rocks had indeed once been a well, and a tall and sturdy one at that, though over time it had partially fallen. A long period of time. "It is a well," she said. "Well done."

"Was that a joke?"

"A joke?" The pun hit her. "Oh, *well*. No, it was not a joke." She put her hands on her hips. "I'm serious. Why does this old well matter?"

"The spear is pointing to it."

"Which could be coincidence."

"You sure about that?" he asked. She lifted her shoulders to indicate she was not. "Then let's find out," Harry said. "Get over here and hold my hand."

Only after he made it clear he intended to lean far over the lip of this unstable well, which could be a thousand feet deep, did she dart over to comply. "You have no idea how deep this is," she said.

He had one hand on what constituted the lip of the well, and one hand stretched out back toward her. "Grab my hand," he said again. "This doesn't look stable. Don't want to fall in."

She clenched his hand with both of hers. Hard calluses on his palm scraped her skin. "Tell me what you're doing," she said. His response was to lean over the crumbling edge, forcing her to lean back to counter his weight. One of her feet skidded on the soft grass. "Tell me right now," she repeated. Nothing. Inspiration struck. "Tell me or I'll drop you in the well."

He clenched her hands tighter and it seemed a shock went from his body to hers. Thank goodness he was listening. She craned her ear toward him, or what was left of him, given his torso was mostly inside the black hole.

"I was right."

The muffled words echoed against the interior of the well. Lauren shook her head. "What did you say?" she asked. He said it again, louder this time. "About what?" she asked, exasperation in every word. This American was getting heavy, and if she dropped him, there was no chance she'd be able to get him out.

She went still. *I could do it right now.* The thought vanished as soon as it appeared. No, she couldn't do it. She wouldn't drop a man down a well and leave him to die. Tom O'Connor might. And Maurice Keane—he'd do it without question. Lauren was not either of them, though Harry Fox didn't know that. Or them, for that matter. "Tell me what in the world you're talking about or I'll—*whoa.*"

She nearly did drop him when Harry ripped himself up and out of the well without warning. A strand of green algae hung from his fingertips. "I found it," he said.

"Found *what*?"

He flicked his hand and the algae went flying. "Proof I'm right. Aed's spear stone is more than a stone. It's a direction, and it's telling us to look in this well."

"How could you possibly prove that?"

"By finding an identical image inside the well." He stuck his hand out. "Want to see for yourself?"

She nearly took his hand before a look at the gaping black maw of the crumbling well convinced her otherwise. "What did you see?" she asked in a softer tone. "Is there a message with the spear?"

Harry shook his head. "Better than a message. The spear image is pointing down. And guess what it points to." He didn't give her a chance. "A ledge. There's a ledge right below it. A ledge you can stand on."

Her sense of adventure vanished. "You cannot go down that well."

"The ledge is in front of an opening in the well." He touched her arm, his fingers still wet from the slime. "It's an entrance. There's a doorway down there. A doorway we can walk through."

Chapter 10

*K*ealkill Circle, County Cork

Lauren made him prove it.

Harry had told her about the spear image inside the well, the ledge he thought he could stand on, and the doorway he suspected was in there. Lauren didn't call him a liar, didn't seem overly shocked at the idea that a random friend of Harry's could have found this hidden doorway in a well in Ireland and devised a scavenger hunt around it. All of this might have raised a red flag in his mind, but he ignored any suspicions he might have had when she agreed to help him check it out. On one condition. That he first lower a phone down the well to record what waited.

"We cannot blindly go down a crumbling well shaft," she said.

Harry nearly jumped. "We?"

"You don't think I would stay up here after your friend went to all this trouble of creating a treasure hunt, do you?" He had nothing to say to that. For any number of reasons. "I am glad you understand me," she said. "If you go, I go with you. I want to see what's waiting."

How in the world could he argue with that? He tried to come up with a rebuttal and failed spectacularly. "Fine." Harry removed a length of climbing rope from his pack, secured his phone onto it, set it to record, and lowered the device down the well. He dangled it there for a few moments and then pulled it back up, and together he and Lauren peered at the screen, which showed a darkened entrance that most certainly existed.

"It's a passageway," Harry said. "Leading toward the ground beneath the Circle." He detached the phone from the rope and pocketed it. "Want to see what's in there?"

"I do," Lauren said. "Preferably without dying. Do you have more climbing rope?"

Harry did, and using the techniques he'd learned at a Brooklyn climbing gym, he fashioned a rudimentary harness that could theoretically lower two people over the edge of a crumbling well and down to a ledge without having them tumble into the dark hole below. He tested the rope and declared it fit for holding them. "Now we need an anchor," Harry said. "Something heavy."

"How about a car?" Lauren asked. "I can drive down the hillside and park here."

Harry grinned. "What are you waiting for?"

Lauren ran through the grass and in short order had her car parked near the well, close enough that Harry could secure the climbing rope to the frame and still leave plenty of slack for lowering themselves to the ledge inside the well. He looped the rope around his legs and waist. "I'll go first," he said. "I'll unhook myself when I get to the ledge, then you pull the rope back up and slip into the harness." He showed her how to tie it around her waist. "Let the rope out a little at a time," he instructed. "I'll grab your feet when you're low enough. It'll be easy."

Lauren's face made it clear how she felt. "I've never climbed up or down anything before."

"You can do it. Trust me."

He didn't give her a chance to argue. Rope around his torso, butt on the sturdiest of the well's upper stones and pack on his back, he threw one leg over the edge and then the other. "I'm letting all the slack out behind me," he told her. "That way I can control my descent." He mimicked climbing down, hand over hand. "It's not far down to the ledge at all. Go slowly, follow my instructions. You'll be fine."

Her already pale face turned an impressive shade of white. "What if I fall?"

"I'll catch you."

"How do I know you won't miss?"

"Like I said. Trust me."

The white shade only worsened. "This is too dangerous."

Harry shrugged. "You can stay up here. I'll let you know what I find."

That seemed to do it. Again, the little red flag appeared: Why would Lauren risk her neck for a treasure hunt? It seemed odd, but Harry wouldn't. let a little thing like logic worry him, not now. He needed her help, but he couldn't tell her why, so whatever he had to say to make it work would be said. He found a foothold inside the well, turned to face her with his waist hidden behind the stones and let the rope out. It dangled into the inky black below. The stones jiggled as he stood on them, so he kept a tight hold of the rope and let his arms take most of his weight as he took one step down, leaning back so he could lower himself one hand at a time while keeping his feet on the wall for support.

One hand over the other. Down he went, the green fields vanishing as the well rose to surround him, leaving only a circle of darkening blue sky visible overhead. Lauren kept hold of the rope and leaned over the well lip to watch him go. Harry kept his eyes up, never looking down, taking it one hand at a time. A stone fell from beneath his feet when he was about halfway to the ledge. He stopped moving, gripping the rope tight, and listened. It was a long time until he heard a splash below. *Hang tight, Harry.*

He didn't think, didn't do anything but focus on putting one hand after the other as he descended. At last, his feet hit the ledge. "I'm down," he called up after escaping from the harness. "You sure you want to do this?"

His words hadn't stopped echoing off the stone walls before Lauren shouted back in no uncertain terms that she was coming. The rope harness shot past him and soon Lauren was over the side, sliding easily down the well's interior to join him on the ledge. Only after he'd secured the rope so they could get out of this deathtrap did he take the flashlight from his pack and aim the beam into the passageway. One characteristic jumped out.

"It's a tunnel," Harry said. "The walls and ceiling are stone, not dirt."

"Which means this is part of a natural underground chamber," Lauren said. Her face portended trouble when she looked at him. "Give me the flashlight." She grabbed it before he could respond. "Look at the ground. It is stone, too, with damp dirt covering this entrance. Do you know what I see?" Harry said he didn't. "Nothing," Lauren said. "I see nothing but smooth dirt. No footprints. No wheel marks. Nothing to tell me anyone has been down here for a thousand years."

"What's the problem?"

She stuck a finger in his face. "You are lying. Your friend didn't come down this well and hide any treasure. Nobody risks their life for a game. Tell me who you are and why you are here. Tell me right now."

Harry might have been better served to keep his mouth shut. But, for whatever reason, he did not. "It's complicated," Harry said. "And dangerous."

"I'm listening."

He rubbed a hand over his face. *Dad's never going to let me hear the end of this.* His first solo mission, and now he had to tell the truth to a complete stranger? "It started when I found a tablet. Not this one, with the spear on it, but another one."

"Where?" she demanded.

They stood inches apart on a narrow ledge inside an ancient well. Even here, the intensity of her response caught him off guard. "What does it matter where I found it?"

Lauren's mouth quickly opened and closed without a word coming out. She looked at the dark passage, then back to him. "I'm curious, that's all."

Why was she grilling him? "Doesn't matter where I found it. What matters is what it said." He recounted acquiring a tablet—no mention of how—that offered a tantalizing glimpse of a journey that couldn't possibly exist. A tale in Latin about Brigid's temple, the Dinan river and reaching for the Morrigan with Tuatha's courage. Lauren made him repeat the clue verbatim. Then she made him do it again, in Latin this time. "What's it matter?" he asked. "The message isn't the point."

Her response was distant, her eyes unfocused. "Incredible."

What was her deal? "Yes, it's incredible, but listen to what happened in the cave." He recounted narrowly escaping a deadly assortment of safeguards. "That's what you don't understand," Harry finished. "This is real. It's deadly. Whatever's waiting at the end meant a whole lot to the Irish of Brittania."

"My people."

"Yeah, I guess so." He leaned back a fraction. "Are you listening to me?"

She blinked. Whatever had taken hold of her these past minutes let go. "Yes. Forgive me." She shook her head as if to clear her vision. "Your story swept me up."

"Don't lose focus out here or you'll get hurt, Lauren," he said soberly. "I've learned that the hard way."

"You've done this sort of business before?"

"In a manner of speaking." He didn't reveal that his father had taken care of the hard parts until now. "Odds are this passage won't let us walk through without a test. I'll go first. You stay behind me. If anything looks off, call it out. Understand?"

"How will I know what's off?"

He turned to face the dark passage and aimed his light inside. "Trust your gut."

Cobwebs fluttered in the light's powerful beam. The stone walls glistened with moisture. Harry leaned into the tunnel, but did not step forward, and his head nearly scraped the roof. He was not a tall man. "Looks like the tunnel opens up ahead," he said. "It gets wider and taller."

"What are you waiting for?" she asked.

"There's one other thing you should know." He reached into his pocket and removed the scrap of paper that had been secreted in the first tablet's hidden compartment. "This was inside the tablet that led me here."

Lauren read the Latin message aloud in English. "*The Romans come. Do not break the tie between Aed and his father. Should you break it, only by avenging Aed's death will you prove worthy.*"

"Before you ask," Harry said, "I have no idea what it means beyond it being clear Romans were invading. The only other thing I took from it was more proof Aed's spear was the right thing to look for. It's what made me certain Kealkill Circle was the correct location."

"Do you know who this message talks about?" Lauren asked.

"You're the scholar. You tell me."

"You are very unprepared for a treasure hunter." She handed the scrap back to him. "You are correct about the Romans. As to the rest, we know Aed is god of the underworld. He is the son of Lir, a sea god who is quite powerful in our mythology."

"What sort of tie did they have, and how do we avoid breaking it?"

"I have no idea."

"I could have come up with that answer."

"It may be the answer will present itself," she said. "In the tunnel."

She tried to move ahead. He put out a hand to stop her. "Tell me about the second part. How can I prove my worth by avenging Aed's death? Sounds like that could be important."

"Aed had an affair with the wife of a man named Corrgend, who killed Aed because of it."

"I thought Aed was a god. How does a man kill a god?"

"Stop asking questions and listen. Corrgend killed Aed. That's what matters. Myths aren't always clear, but on this matter, the issue is well defined. You prove your worth by delivering vengeance on Corrgend for having killed Aed."

And he thought he'd been confused before. "That still makes no sense." He turned to the tunnel. "We'll figure it out later. Stay behind me. Don't touch anything. Understand?"

Lauren said she did, so Harry took a careful look at the floor and walls of the tunnel before setting one foot inside. Nothing happened, so he took another step, and then another. Stone surrounded him on all sides. Unmarked stone. "You see anything I'm missing?" he asked.

"Marks on the walls, booby-trapped floors, that sort of thing." Lauren said she did not. "Me neither," he said.

Quit stalling. Dry air scraped at his throat as he walked into the tunnel. The distant noise of water moving far below gave a pressing reminder that untold tons of earth and stone were above him, while a watery tomb waited behind and below. Humans had not walked this path for two thousand years. Harry had no idea what waited.

"They wanted someone to come here." He said it to himself as much as Lauren. "The path they left was meant to be followed."

"Then why leave traps to try and kill anyone who came past?" Lauren asked.

"As protection. Somehow that first tablet never made it to the right person."

"Who was?"

"A person who believed in Irish mythology. A person who could resurrect those beliefs after the Romans came through. We can guess the ancient Irish wanted to protect their beliefs instead of having them co-opted or destroyed. This path is part of that protection."

"Which suggests there is something very valuable to find."

"Any idea what it is?" he asked.

"I have an idea, but we will wait and see."

He had just opened his mouth to press her on the topic when he spotted it. "Look." Harry stopped walking and pointed ahead. "Two carvings. One on each side of the wall. Right after the tunnel opens up." The tight tunnel widened and the ceiling rose ahead. He aimed his light at the carving to their left. "It's bigger than me," he said. "Looks like a warrior. Do you—"

"He's from the story of Aed." Lauren came to stand beside him. "That's Corrgend."

"The one who killed Aed?"

"Yes," she said. "You can tell by the axe he carries and the sash looped over his chest."

The carving depicted a seven-foot-tall man with long, plaited hair who had a giant axe resting on one shoulder. Half his chest could be seen beneath what Lauren called a sash, though to Harry it resembled a toga on top, with some sort of metal kilt at the waist that reached halfway down his thighs. His biceps were the stuff of legend. Harry flicked his light to the carving directly across from Corrgend. "This other guy on the right wall looks an awful lot like Corrgend. Who is he?"

This carving appeared much the same as the first. Big muscles, a toga-like sash, the metal kilt. Instead of an axe, this man had a spear resting on his shoulder. Other than that, they were identical. "Look by his foot," Harry said. "There's a circle carved in the wall." The circle reached to this new man's knee. "Any idea what that is?"

Harry stepped forward. He was too focused on the new carving to note that Lauren had stepped up, then kept going to get a better look. The hair on his neck rose, an electric pulse shot up his body, but he hesitated a moment. A moment too long.

"I don't know—whoops."

Lauren stumbled as she neared the wall. A metallic *twang* filled the air, as though a guitar string had been plucked. A thin string flashed like metal in Harry's light when he looked at the floor, and before he could blink a thunderous roar filled the air and iron rained down from the heavens.

Air *whooshed*, a chain rumbled and dust exploded all around them. Harry had no time to react before an iron cage encircled them both.

His flashlight went flying as Lauren leapt at him, screaming as she wrapped her arms around his torso. Harry twisted loose, grabbed her by the shoulders and held tight. "Stand still," he ordered. She listened.

He let go with one hand to bend down and grab his flashlight, which had landed by his foot. The light flickered off a million tiny crystals as the dust cloud around them settled and the *bang* of the crashing cage finally faded. "Are you hurt?" he asked.

"What just happened?"

He aimed his light at the floor. "Looks like you broke a tripwire." He bent down. "Bronze. This thing has been here for a long time."

"Why in the world would they have a tripwire in here?"

Harry stayed kneeling as he aimed his light at one wall, then the other. Two more images had been carved into the wall at ground level, low and small, each of them no bigger than the cover of a novel. "Recognize that guy?" He pointed at one picture. "Looks an awful lot like a picture of Aed I saw when I read about him."

Lauren's composure returned. "It's Aed." She knelt beside him. "One of the classical depictions from ancient times. The long mustache, the short beard, a massive sword."

"Care to guess who's on the other side?" He moved his light to illuminate the other carving. "I don't have any idea what he's supposed to look like, but my guess is that's Aed's father."

"Lir," Lauren said. "The sea god." She stood, and Harry joined her. "The message warned us. I missed it." She turned to face him. "I broke the tie between Aed and his father. I'm so sorry."

Harry could have panicked. He could have shouted. Instead of either option, he closed his eyes. An image of his father came to mind, and his father was speaking. *Don't lose your head in the field. Deal with one problem at a time. You'll live longer that way.*

"I missed it too," is what he said. He had also not gone running ahead without looking, but he didn't voice that thought. His light played over the iron bars. "This is one big bird cage. There must be a way out of here. What else did the message say?" He thought for a moment. "Only by avenging Aed's death will we prove ourselves worthy."

Lauren grabbed the thick iron bars and heaved on them to no effect. "What in the world does that mean?"

Harry grabbed the bars and pulled along with her. They may as well have tried to move a Cadillac. "Something to do with that Corrgend guy is my guess." He heaved again; nothing happened. A noise caught his ear. "Don't move." Harry put a hand on her arm to stay her. "Do you hear that?"

Lauren fell silent as Harry turned an ear toward the right wall. An odd noise came from behind it. A liquid noise, a gurgling sound he associated with water running through pipes hidden behind walls. "It sounds like water moving," Harry said. "Do you hear it too?"

"I do." Lauren's hand shot out and nearly took his nose off. "Look, by the floor."

A hole neither of them had seen before began spurting dark liquid that oozed rather than flowed, moving at a steady clip toward the bottom of the cage around them. Harry watched as more liquid came out of the hole, accelerating the growth of the puddle, which now reached the edge of the cage and began to creep through the bars.

A pungent aroma filled the air. "It stinks," Lauren said. "What is it?"

"It's not oil," Harry said. "But it sure looks like it." The acrid, greasy smell seemed to coat the inside of his nose. "I bet that stuff's flammable. Do you have any jewelry on?" he asked. Lauren said no. "Good. You wouldn't want to hit the iron bars and make a spark. Do that and we'll be on fire."

They were in no danger of drowning, but a sense of impending doom he'd felt a few times now on this relic hunt flashed to life once more in his gut. This dark, viscous liquid did not bode well for them.

He aimed his light around the cage and was rewarded with a flash from above. "What's that?" He reached up and discovered the metallic flash was indeed metal. Metal with a long wooden pole attached to it.

"A spear," Lauren said. "It's attached to the top. I think you can pull it down."

He reached up and removed the spear from where it hung horizontally inside the cage. "There are hooks for it," Harry said. "This was left here on purpose."

"As part of the message?" Lauren guessed. "The end, where it mentions avenging Aed's death?"

Use this spear to avenge the death of a god? It made no sense. Not because it was lunacy, but because he didn't understand it yet. *Think.* "This spear is here for a reason," Harry said. "It's the only thing inside this cage. This is our ticket out of this mess."

Lauren wasn't listening. "The liquid's puddling in here."

He looked down to find a growing pool of the goop around his feet, contained enough by the cage that they were in it up to their ankles now. "I noticed."

"I don't like this, Harry. This is a trap. We're stuck, and whoever set this isn't done yet."

Exactly what worried him. "Focus on the spear," he said. "How can we use this to avenge a murdered god?" He drew oily air in through his nose. "Vengeance. Aed must be avenged, which means we need to deal with his killer." Harry's eyes widened. "Corrgend. The guy who killed Aed. He's right there." Harry pointed at the right wall. "Or maybe over there." Harry pointed at the left wall. "Which one is it?"

"This is crazy." Lauren's voice grew louder. "Those are stone carvings, not people. You can't do anything to them with a spear."

Harry aimed his light at the carving on the right. It had to be here. A clue, a marker, something he was missing. The answer to this opaque riddle. Two nearly identical men, one with an axe, the other with a spear. Nothing else differentiated them. *Wait.* "The circle."

Lauren turned her gaze from the flowing, treacly substance to Harry. "What circle?"

"The one by that guy's ankle. The guy with the spear. There's a circle by his ankle. Some kind of symbol. Or maybe it's a rock."

That got Lauren's attention. "A rock."

Harry was about to respond when a new noise caught his ear. A crackling noise, undercut by a low rumble. It came from further down the tunnel. Harry looked ahead, into a darkness that wasn't so dark anymore. "Oh, no."

The passageway walls had come alive. Shadows flickered across them as the faint rumbling grew louder. The once-black walls were turning burnt orange and the crackling sound rose in volume as he watched. A primal fear filled his body as the world focused into a single point of moving light. A circular object rolling down the tunnel came into view. Heavy enough to make his toes vibrate. Fast enough that it wouldn't stop. A rolling object engulfed in flames.

Lauren stared at it with her mouth agape. "That will set this cage on fire," she said. "Stop it with that spear. Harry, get the spear over there now."

"It's not long enough." Batting the fiery ball aside with his spear wouldn't matter if it touched the pool of black liquid, a pool whose edge was already farther out than his spear could reach. "It'll hit this black stuff before I knock it away," he said. "That's not the answer."

"Then what do we do?" Her voice had become a soft shriek, almost too high to hear. "We're going to die."

Not if I can help it. He forced his gaze off the rolling ball of doom and onto the walls. First the right wall, then the left. Axe man on the left, spear man on the right. One had a boulder beside him. Two nearly identical men. That's where their salvation would be found. *The answer is right in front of you. Find it.*

"Which one is Corrgend?" Harry asked. "Quickly, please."

The words poured out of her mouth. "Corrgend was a hunter," she said. "Or a warrior. The stories vary."

"That's not helpful. What else?" He glanced at the ball growing ever closer. They had ten seconds. "Look at their chests," Harry said. "They each have some kind of emblem on their sash. A circle. What does that mean?"

"Nothing I recognize." She grabbed the bars. "It's not a decoration I know."

Not a decoration. What else could it be? The ball rolled closer and he had the answer. "It's a target." He looked at the spear. "And this is how you press it. You avenge Aed's death by throwing this spear at his killer. Right at the target."

"Throw it," Lauren shouted.

"Which one?"

The rolling ball left a trail of flame in its wake. Accelerant on its stony surface crackled and popped. The tunnel was now awash in bright, flickering light. "I don't know," Lauren said. "Corrgend's legend is about him dying when he—*the boulder.* That's a boulder by his foot. Throw it at the one with a spear!"

Harry didn't think. He reacted, pulling the spear back, taking aim between the cage bars and hurling it at the target on the carving with a spear and a boulder by its foot. He'd played lots of baseball growing up. Did that translate into throwing spears? The wooden shaft left his fingers, flew through the air toward the carving that was too far to reach from inside the cage, and as the roar of the burning orb bore down on them, the spear flew and their lives hung in the balance.

"You hit it!"

Lauren's voice filled the passage as his spear smashed into the circular target, pushing that section of the wall in on itself. The spear bounced off and hit the rolling inferno, then fell to the ground.

Dust and rock exploded in front of them. A blockade erupted from the tunnel floor, a barricade that stretched from wall to wall springing up to waist height, blocking the burning ball just inches before it reached the black liquid. The ball clattered off the stone barrier and bounced back so they could see only the flames but not the ball itself. They could still hear the crackle of burning accelerant as it rolled against the wall and moved no further.

"You did it," Lauren said. "You saved us." She reached out and grabbed the iron bars for support. The bars fell open under her touch. "It's a door," she said. "You must have unlocked this door."

Harry pushed her through and followed right behind. "I'm not waiting around for that to close again." His boots squelched in the oozy black goop as he moved to lean over the wall and look down at the burning ball that had nearly roasted them alive. "It's coated in accelerant," he confirmed. "It'll burn itself out in a minute."

Lauren coughed as black smoke began filling the air. "Is the spear over there?" she asked, pointing over the barrier. Harry said it was. "Lean over and grab it. Push the ball aside." She coughed again.

"I'll leave that to you." His fingers wouldn't stop shaking, his heart wouldn't slow down. Harry backed away from the thickening smoke and put his back to the wall. He slid down, landed on his butt, and leaned his head back, resting his hands on the ground. One finger ran over a smooth wire. The metallic string Lauren had broken. "Should have paid closer attention," he told himself as he closed his eyes. "Remember that next time."

Lauren took his advice and let the ball burn itself out. Meanwhile, she told him about the legend of Aed, and how Corrgend had been cursed by the gods and tasked with finding a tombstone for Aed after killing him. A tombstone that proved so heavy it burst Corrgend's heart when he lifted it. Harry thanked her for the story. He did not say anything about speaking faster next time. Make peace, not war.

"You still glad you came down here?" Harry asked. The smoke stung his eyes and made him cough.

"I am."

"Why?"

He did not expect her response. "Because this is my country," she said. "And it's worth saving."

That made him turn to look at her. "Saving from what?"

"From *whom*. You've stumbled on a mystery about the old gods. The gods of our ancestors." Her voice dropped and he had to strain to catch it. "Gods we perhaps should not have forgotten. Gods who wanted more for our people."

This was interesting. "More what? Sacrifices?"

A joke. One she did not appreciate. "The Irish didn't have sacrificial practices in their religion." A pause. "Not many, at least, which is not the point. What I mean is more care about the people. A leader who knows them, who wants the best for them." Her face darkened to match the growing gloom on the walls. "Not for himself."

"I'm guessing you don't like politicians." Lauren's expression indicated she did not. "You prefer a king?" he asked half-jokingly. "You know what they say about absolute power."

"Remind me."

"It corrupts absolutely."

"Only if the king is a bad one. We had good kings once. Long ago. We could have them again."

She lapsed into a silence Harry decided to join. In a few minutes' time, the rock stopped burning and they were up and over the waist-high barrier that had saved their lives before heading deeper into the passage. A passage, he discovered, that had one more surprise.

"It ends up there," Harry said. "There's a room." He narrowed his gaze. "And guess what's inside?"

To his slight surprise, Lauren did not run into the room. She must have learned her lesson in the passage earlier. A true show of restraint, for before them now was the reason behind the ancient Irish having left a deadly trap in this passage.

A tablet, sitting atop a pedestal. A tablet with Latin writing on it.

Chapter 11

Lauren reached for the controls on Harry's dashboard and flicked the heat on. "It gets cold here when the sun goes down," she said. "I didn't plan on being here this late."

A half-moon had not yet fully risen above the plains as they sat in Harry's car, still parked outside the single gate on the path leading to Kealkill Circle. The western horizon remained purpled from a sun now fallen from view. "Are you sure it's safe to stay here?" Harry asked from the driver's seat. "I don't want to spend the night in an Irish jail cell."

"Yes, it's fine." Lauren said it with a conviction that almost made Harry believe her. "This is a public road. They'd hardly put you in jail for sitting in your car."

He grunted an acknowledgment. Being trapped in that cage and nearly roasted alive had left a nervous energy in his bones that showed no sign of dissipating. He'd been all nerves when they entered the chamber at the end of the tunnel, jumping at each crack and echo when he removed the third tablet from the simple pedestal. Lauren had demanded she be allowed to carry it out as they backtracked down the passageway, past the iron cage and goopy accelerant, though she'd let Harry store the tablet in his pack as he climbed the rope back to the surface, then pulled her up in turn. He had ignored her questions about the Latin inscription on the tablet until they were safely back in his car, the engine running, ready for a getaway. Only with that veneer of security around him did he address the new challenge at hand.

"What do you make of it?" he asked Lauren.

"That's what I've been asking you," she fired back. The tablet lay between them. "I want an outside perspective."

"You mean an uninformed one." He grinned to soften the retort.

"Hardly. You made it farther than anyone has for two millennia."

A fair compliment. "Fine. I'll go first. The inscription is in Latin, same as the others." He read it aloud, likely butchering the ancient mythical names. "*Stand before Nuada's lost arm and look to where Danu arrives across Manann's home.*" He looked up at her. "Did I say that properly?"

"That's what I'm reading."

"Care to tell me who these people are?"

"Each is from Irish mythology. Nuada is the first king of the Tuatha Dé Danann. Danu is a goddess belonging to the same supernatural race of beings, though to be completely open, the stories around her are not consistent in their content."

"And Manann?"

"A sea god. Also one of the Tuatha."

Harry pointed at each name on the tablet in turn. "Nuada, Danu, Manann. Their stories are key. That will tell us where to go next. More importantly, what to expect. First, where did Nuada lose an arm?" She opened her mouth. "And how?" Harry quickly asked. "Tell me the story. It could matter. There could be a message in the story we need to know."

"As I said, it's lucky you have me here."

"Are all Irish ladies this humble?"

That got a proper chuckle out of her. "Most are worse," Lauren said. "As I said, Nuada was the first king of the Tuatha. The Tuatha required their king to be physically perfect—don't ask me why—which Nuada was until he lost an arm in combat. Later, it would be replaced with a silver arm, thus allowing him to become king once again."

"Where did he lose the arm?"

"At a mythical battle that allegedly took place in what is now County Mayo, at or near the village of Cong." She shrugged. "At least that's what most people believe."

Great. His guide would be a fictional tale about a race of mythical beings who battled in a place no one could quite identify. What could go wrong? "Please tell me there's a massive statue in Cong of Nuada's lost arm."

"No such luck." She reached out and adjusted the heater, then put a hand on her chin. "I can't recall any monuments or locations tied to Nuada around Cong."

Which didn't mean none existed. "We can figure that out later. Any stone circles at all? They've helped before." Again, she said no. "Okay, moving on. Where does Danu arrive?"

"That part is easy," Lauren said. "Danu is a goddess most closely tied to successful crops and rebirth in general. What signifies rebirth and also helps crops grow?"

This was Deciphering Ancient Clues 101. "The sun," Harry said. "The tablet is telling us to look east."

"To where Danu arrives with the rising sun. I agree." The dashboard's glow cast her face in shadow as she pointed to the last few Latin words. "The final section is about Manann. He is a sea god. If what we seek is near water, we would be wise to look there."

A god without an arm. Look to the east, hopefully near water. Harry couldn't make heads or tails of it, not without more research.

He rubbed the stubble on his chin. "I have to make a phone call," he said abruptly. "I need a minute."

Lines creased Lauren's forehead as Harry got out of the car without speaking, taking his pack as he closed the door and walking a short distance away. He didn't know what the tablet was trying to say. He did know who to ask. He just didn't want to admit who that was to Lauren. Not yet. He dialed a number and put the phone to his ear, listening to it ring.

"It must be getting late in Ireland."

"Hi, Dad." Harry ran a hand through his hair. "It is. You have a second?"

"I hoped you might call with a status update."

"Then you're in luck." Harry recapped his trip to Kealkill Circle, deciphering the mystery around Aed's spear and finding the underground passageway by descending into an ancient well. Fred preempted him on the trap.

"Did you run across anything interesting inside the passage?" Harry gave a slightly sanitized version of the cage and spear test. "I see," Fred said. "It seems those years spent teaching you to play baseball were more useful than I realized."

"That's one way to put it," Harry said. "But here's the best part. We found a new tablet?"

"We?"

Darn it. "I found," Harry said quickly. "I found a new tablet. That's three new ones in total. Sorry, I'm trying to do two things at once. Listen to what is written on it."

If Fred suspected anything, he didn't say it. "Written in Latin again?" Fred asked.

Harry said it was before reciting the message from memory. *"Stand before Nuada's lost arm and look to where Danu arrives across Manann's home."*

"Any idea what it means?" Fred asked. Harry gave a summary of Nuada, the king who lost an arm in a mythical battle that may or may not have happened near a village called Cong. "Only one way to find out if that's true," Fred said. "You'll need to visit the village."

"I'm headed there soon," Harry said. "Danu is another god tied to the sun, which tells me to look east. Manann is a sea god from Irish mythology." A fact that, Harry realized, represented the entirety of his knowledge on the god. "I'm still researching that last one."

"All logical interpretations," Fred said. "Well done, Harry. Well done indeed. Impressive thinking on your feet."

A pleasant warmth came to life in his body. "Thanks," Harry said. "Didn't have much of a choice."

"You acted," Fred said. "You didn't freeze, didn't run. However, one piece of advice. Know when to run, and know when you could use a hand."

"I'm fine, Dad." A mechanical noise sounded behind him and Harry looked over his shoulder. Lauren stood outside of his car. "One second." Harry put the call on mute. "What's wrong?" Harry asked.

"Nothing," Lauren said. "Have to grab something out of my car."

Harry nodded and took his call off mute. "I'm back. You see anything I'm missing in the message?"

"Nothing immediate," Fred said. "You already know to check for memorials or historical ties to Nuada near the village. The sea god reference could be interpreted in several ways. You may find a body of water near the village or a location tied to Nuada, and you'll need to look near the water, of course. It could also be a location or object specifically related to Manann, or part of his story. It's hard to say until you decipher the business with Nuada's lost arm."

"Those were pretty much my thoughts as well." A beeping came from near his car. He looked back to find Lauren had returned from her vehicle and was now climbing back into his passenger seat. "Appreciate the advice," Harry said. "I'm headed out now."

"To Cong?" Fred asked. "It's late. Get some sleep first. Whatever's waiting will still be there in the morning."

Harry said he would think about it, which he didn't mean, and he said he'd call Fred when he knew more, which he did. Fred knew all this and didn't push it. "I'll see you soon," Fred said. The line went dead.

Harry opened a navigation map on his phone and input the destination. A village called Cong waited several hundred kilometers north of where he was now. If that was even where he needed to go. "I'm not driving four hours just to find that out," he muttered. Grass painted purple by the moonlight rustled beneath his feet as he walked back to the running car. A light glowed from inside Lauren's car.

"You left your car on," Harry said as he opened the driver's door on his vehicle and slid inside. "Don't want a dead battery."

She didn't look at him when she responded. "It will turn off by itself."

"Okay." He showed her his phone. "Cong is about four hours north of here. I don't want to drive up there until we know more. I could be missing something. I need to do more research." He hesitated. "Where do you live, anyway? I might need a hotel for the night and have no clue what's around here."

"Dublin," she said. "But I'm from a small town just like this one. There should be an inn close by. A town this size will have one." She still hadn't looked at him.

"What do you think?" he asked. "About Cong. Is that where you would go?"

Lauren made a sound indicating she was far from committed. "Did your call shed any light on the question?" she asked.

Fishing for information. He wasn't biting. "A little," Harry said. "Mainly I know that I need to know more before I act."

"Does the person you called know what you're doing?" she asked. "I hope you can trust them."

"Yes, they do, and yes, I can." He flipped the subject. "Doesn't matter anyway. I'm in this alone."

That got a reaction. "Alone?" she said, looking at him now.

Oops. "Not alone. You're here, but it's just me. You and me. We got this." He offered a half-grin. "Trust me."

She didn't smile, only shook her head once. "I do." Her shoulders went up, and then down. "What if there is another angle running through the message of each tablet?"

That got his attention. "Such as?"

"The Midsummer holiday. The tablet from the Dunmore Caves led you to a stone circle, which led to a second stone circle. Many circles tie back to the Midsummer celebration."

"Stone circles are often constructed in specific locations that tie to the sun rising on specific days or in certain locations," Harry said. "I can't argue with that. Is there a stone circle near Cong?"

She ignored him and gazed out the window again. "First the Romans tried to conquer Brittania. Rome's history of assimilating the cultures of conquered peoples made their new subjects more accepting of their Roman overlords. We know the Romans turned the Irish pagan Midsummer celebration into a festival honoring their goddess Fortuna, then the Christians repurposed the same idea into the Feast of Saint John. After the Romans stopped executing them, of course."

Lauren looked through the windshield at a starry sky, though he suspected her gaze was focused on something even more distant than those dots of light. "Stolen, over and over, until no one remembers what it used to be." She turned to face him. "The bad guys nearly w on."

Where was she going with this? "Nearly?"

"Nearly, but not yet." Her mouth tightened. "It was fateful, wouldn't you say? Us running into each other today."

He was still trying to figure out where she was going with the whole idea of Midsummer being stolen. Toss in her earlier fervor about an Irish king and people not being represented and she'd done a darn good job of confusing him. "I guess so," he said, only half-listening. "What was it you said about a king earlier?"

"A king?" She smiled at that. "I'll explain in a moment. May I see the tablet again?" she asked. Harry handed it over. "I have an idea. But I need to get something else out of my car first." She put a hand on his bicep and squeezed gently. "Be right back."

She hopped out of her seat and went to her car. Harry watched but didn't really see her; his mind was churning. A cool breeze snuck through the door she'd left partially open as he ran through the Lauren-related aspects of today. A scholar presented with this once-in-a-lifetime opportunity to join a treasure hunt. Lauren had been awed, sure, and scared at times, as expected. Yet she'd only seemed truly and fully alive at two points that day. The first was when she'd been speaking about the Irish people not being represented, suggesting that times had been better when a king lorded over the island. The second was just now. Her voice hadn't risen, her tone hadn't hardened, yet he could see it all the same. The same passion she'd felt when talking about Ireland's royal past came through loud and clear when she'd told him of the stolen pagan Midsummer.

A soft beeping that had been sounding since Lauren got out finally intruded on his thoughts. "She didn't shut the door." Harry reached over to shut it. The beeping was annoying, but the cool breeze coming through the open door had become downright chilly. He looked over and saw that Lauren was sitting in the driver's seat of her car; the tail-lights were now on. Probably couldn't find whatever she needed and had turned the car on for light, he thought. Harry pulled the passenger door shut. The interior light winked off and the breeze stopped. The beeping noise continued. "Why won't that beeping stop?"

He didn't have a chance to inspect his dashboard for the reason before the squeal of tires spinning on grass grabbed his ear. Lauren's car fishtailed, nearly smacking his front end before her tires caught and dirt flew. A thick cloud of it shrouded her car, painted red by her taillights and then dwindling as she raced away. Harry's car was already running. He shoved the gearshift into drive and smashed the gas pedal.

Nothing happened. Blue language filled the car as he tried again. What was going on? A light flashed on his dashboard and the incessant beeping continued. Lauren veered around a corner ahead and zipped out of sight. He jabbed the start button to turn the engine off and on, slammed the shifter back to park and then to drive once more before mashing his foot down on the gas. Nothing. No engine, no lights, nothing. Why won't this car—*oh no.*

"She took my keys." That's why the car wouldn't turn back on. Lauren had taken his key fob when she went to her car. The fob had been in his center console. A console now filled with nothing but air. Harry grabbed the wheel with both hands, considered trying to rip it loose, then let go. *I turned the engine off and I can't restart it.* The air rushed from his chest as he sank into his seat. Lauren had the tablet. She knew everything he knew. He had been bamboozled, and every second he spent stuck in this useless car was another second she moved closer to the truth while Harry fell back. The glow of her red taillights against the dark summer sky faded away as he sat watching helplessly. How long he sat there he couldn't say. One minute. Perhaps two. That's how long it took him to muster the courage to do what had to be done. *He's never going to let me forget this.*

He pulled out his phone, punched in the number, and waited, his lips pursed, until it connected. "I have a problem," he said.

Fred Fox did not sound concerned. "What's the matter?"

Harry recounted the past few minutes. Fred didn't interrupt, didn't get upset, didn't do anything but listen. The silence stretched on for several seconds after Harry stopped speaking. Long enough that Harry spoke again. "Any advice would be appreciated."

"Don't trust strangers," Fred said. "And tell me exactly where you are."

"Sitting in a useless car beside the Kealkill Stone Circle." He rubbed one eye with the palm of his hand. "I made a mistake. A big one."

Fred's laughter made Harry sit up in his chair. "You think you're the first person to have the wool pulled over your eyes?" Fred asked. "It happens to the best of us. Even me."

"You?" Harry asked. "When?"

"A story for another time," Fred said. "Don't beat yourself up over this, son. Everyone makes mistakes. That doesn't matter. What does matter is how you respond. Do you let this be the end of the story, or simply the end of a chapter? I know which option I'd choose."

The air returned to his lungs. So the mighty Fred Fox had stumbled before, too, perhaps been hoodwinked or tripped up on a relic hunt, and he had come out on the other end. Fred Fox, the man who found relics for the largest crime family in New York. If Fred could bounce back, so could Harry. "The latter," Harry replied. "This book isn't over yet."

"Good man," Fred said. "Now sit still. We'll be back on her tail in an hour."

Harry sat up so fast he hit his head on the roof. "We?"

"That's right," Fred replied. "You didn't think I'd let you have all the fun in Ireland, did you? I landed in Dublin this afternoon. I'm sixty minutes from Kealkill."

Harry found his brain had taken a coffee break. "You are?"

"Take a quick nap," Fred told him. "You need a clear head. You and I are going after a pagan treasure. Don't worry, Harry. The chase is just getting started."

Chapter 12

Uragh Circle, County Kerry

Turns out Lauren had a sense of humor.

Harry's stolen car keys had been hanging on the *Kealkill Stone Circle* site signage when Fred Fox arrived. Fred tossed his son the keys when he pulled up. "Good morning, son." His breath frosted the air.

Harry was in no mood for pleasantries. "You didn't have to come."

"I know." A half-moon backlit Fred's face as he walked over to Harry and put an arm around the younger man's shoulders. "I wanted to come. Can't pass up a chance to have some fun with you."

"Not much fun right now."

Fred squeezed Harry's shoulder before stepping back. He stood a head taller than his son. "Then let's change that. Chin up, Harry. Everybody falls. Not everyone gets back up. Be one who does."

He'd heard enough of his dad's pep talks over the years that those words could have gone in one ear and out the other. Mostly they did. Today, though, he needed to hear it more than he'd ever admit. "What makes you think I'm not back on my feet already?"

Fred dipped his chin. "That's my boy. Get me up to speed. The clock is ticking."

Harry wasn't much for hugs, but he could have embraced his dad right now. A cool flame lit in his gut. "Right," he said. "Here's what I know."

He recapped the events of what had now become yesterday, from Lauren arriving at the site to him identifying the well and its hidden spear marker, which led to the subterranean tunnel and the incident with the falling cage. Fred perked up—not at that, but when Harry described the tablet waiting at the passage end. "You said it was in Latin," Fred said. Harry told him this was true. "Which you read fluently," Fred replied. "No chance you misinterpreted the message?"

"No chance." Years toiling under tutors and his father's eye to absorb the archaic language had left Harry as fluent as any scholar. "*Stand before Nuada's lost arm and look to where Danu arrives across Manann's home,*" he said.

"This Lauren woman suggested Nuada's arm was potentially lost in the vicinity of what is now a village called Cong?" Fred asked.

"That's what she said. I haven't verified anything yet."

"Putting Cong aside for the moment, are there any themes or consistencies among the locations where you have discovered tablets?"

Harry considered. First a cave and a bridge. Then a stone circle and a castle. Most recently, a stone circle and a well. "Other than all these sites being ancient? Stone circles. That's the only recurring aspect. If you can even call two incidents 'recurring.'"

"Nothing else?" Harry said no. "Then we would be wise to factor that into our plans," Fred said. "The ancient Irish left a path that was meant to be followed. Using objects with permanence, like stone circles, made it more likely any messages or directions they wanted to be found would still exist when whoever followed this trail came through."

"Which means we're looking for a stone circle."

"I'm not saying it's certain, but it's a good place to start." Fred winked at Harry. "Trust me. I've done this a few times."

More than a few, Harry suspected. Stories for later, after Harry had one of his own to tell. "I don't know enough about stone circles or Irish mythology to say if there's a connection between the gods from this last message and any circles."

Fred leaned his backside against Harry's car and crossed his arms. "I used to go to the library to answer those sorts of questions. In the spirit of all older people complaining about younger people, I will tell you how lucky you are that cell phones exist and can answer most any question."

Harry pulled his phone out. "If you have a good signal, that is. I have one bar here."

"Then what do you suggest we do?"

Harry started. "Me?"

"Yes, you. This is your relic hunt. You're in charge. What do we do now?"

This felt like a test. Harry had always tested well in school, but the stakes here were far different. Yes, death and danger and all that, but the highest stake of all came from who was asking the question. Fred Fox was good at what he did. Some would say he was the best. That's why Vincent Morello and the Morello family embraced Fred as their own. Harry often felt as though he were tagging along for the ride. He didn't have the respect of many Morello family members, including the ones his own age. Vincent Morello's son, Joey, had always maintained a distance when it came to dealing with Harry. The baseball games and boxing matches in local gyms had never completely thawed the relationship between the two boys, who were now young men. Any thaw, Harry suspected, would only happen when he proved he was more than just Fred Fox's son.

I'm in charge? Then let's do this. "We get in your car and drive to town," Harry said. He forced a confidence into his voice he didn't quite feel. "There's better reception in town. Find a connection between Nuada, Danu or Manann and a stone circle, and we know where to go." He hesitated. "Which may or may not be the village of Cong."

"Well done," Fred said. "Mostly that last part where you let go of your presupposition. Let the evidence guide your feelings, not the other way round."

Fred started walking toward his car.

"What about using my gut?" Harry asked before starting to follow. "You always say to trust it. My gut says Cong is the right place. Odds are that's where Lauren is headed."

Fred didn't stop walking, didn't turn around. "You'll figure that part out on your own," he called over a shoulder. "By doing one thing."

"What's that?" Harry asked.

"Getting experience." Fred stopped beside his driver's-side door. "Which you don't get by standing around. Come on. We're headed to town."

Harry followed Fred for ten minutes until Fred stopped his vehicle near the middle of the first town they came to. Cell phone reception was strong, and it took Harry all of two minutes of feverishly working his phone to prove Fred's point. "It's not Cong," Harry said from the passenger seat of his father's car. "A stone circle in County Kerry has a picture tied to Nuada."

Fred sat behind the wheel, his seat reclined, eyes closed. "How so?" he asked without opening his eyes.

"One stone in the circle has an image of Nuada's lost arm engraved on it."

"Is that so?" Fred opened one eye. "I'd say that's worth checking out."

"Let's go."

Fred's only move was to close his eye again. "You're certain that's the only connection worth checking out?"

Harry's thoughts churned. "No?"

"You don't sound confident."

What was his dad getting at? Time to throw some of Fred's own advice back at him. "Nothing's certain in the field."

Fred laughed. "No fair using my own words against me."

"Then tell me what the heck you're getting at."

"I want to make sure you're being thorough."

"How thorough are you when you do this?"

"Thorough enough that I feel confident in my decision."

"That's less than helpful," Harry said. Fred didn't bother replying. Harry kept searching for another ten minutes before the tension in his gut, the one true feeling he did have, grew too tight. He put his phone down. "I'm confident," Harry said.

"In your decision?"

"I'm more confident this Lauren woman, whoever she really may be, is getting further ahead of us every minute. It's time to move."

"And if you're wrong about, where was it, County Kerry?"

"It's called Uragh Stone Circle in County Kerry," Harry said. "If I'm wrong, we keep digging." Harry decided to push his luck. "Nobody ever got any experience standing around talking."

This got a chuckle out of Fred. "Now you're learning." He sat up, fixed his seat, and pointed at Harry's vehicle. "Go get your pack and get in."

Harry did as ordered before returning to Fred's car, which took off like a shot when Fred stamped on the gas. Several hours of driving later a road sign announced they had arrived at the outer limits of Glenin-chaquin Park. Fred pulled off the road well back of the entrance. He had doused his headlights at the bottom of a small rise a quarter mile back, navigating the remaining distance by moonlight alone. The sky had cleared, stars pushed back against the endless dark overhead, and Harry narrowed his eyes as he peered toward the park.

Fred spoke first. "Notice anything?"

A black sky pricked with white dots and a heavy moon. The outline of a mountain in the distance. The sound of a body of water not quite at rest off in the distance. "I hear water," Harry said. "The tablet mentioned Danu, the Irish sea god. We need to find a location near water." His chest tightened. "This could be it."

"Good start," Fred said. "Not what I mean. Look again."

It took him several seconds. "Lights. There are lights on in the park." A dim white glow touched the dark horizon ahead. Well ahead, perhaps a quarter mile or more. "That's why you turned the headlights off before we arrived."

"Prepare for the worst," Fred said. "If it turns out you encounter the best, you'll be pleasantly surprised." He lifted a finger. "Which is the only sort of surprise you want in the field." He inclined his head toward the soft glow Harry had missed. "Who do you think is in this specific Irish park in the middle of the night?"

"A park ranger?"

"Doubtful. Try again."

"Someone who's in a hurry and doesn't want other people to know they're here?"

"That was my guess," Fred said. "Do we think this is your new friend Lauren?"

No way. "She went to Cong," Harry said. "That's where the myth-ical battle took place. Cong is hours north of here. There's no way she could have driven all the way to Cong and then come back here." Harry considered what he'd just said. "Unless she never went to Cong at all."

"You identified Uragh Stone Circle as a possibility for the next location," Fred said. "If Lauren really is a scholar, there's no reason she couldn't as well."

"Then why didn't she know about Nuada's arm carving right away?"

"Ireland is a big country with lots of stone circles. Perhaps she didn't know about the carving," Fred said. "Or perhaps she misled you all along."

Harry could only shake his head. He had to get over the idea Lauren had been honest about anything. Her being at Kealkill was no chance. It couldn't be, not with what had transpired. "How could she have known I would be there?" he asked. "She wasn't at the Fal Stone."

"Hard to say," Fred replied. "I've found there are often more people involved in fieldwork than you realize. Your activities at the cave complex must have been noticed. It's possible she, or someone she knows, tracked you based on that."

"Nobody saw me there."

"Correction. *You* didn't see anyone. That doesn't mean no one saw *you*. Or this could be exactly what it appears to be: a scholar who saw her chance and took it. It's hard to say why, and until you know more, it's irrelevant. We believe we're in the correct location. Someone else is here as well. Deal with what's in front of you and worry about the rest later."

"Fine," Harry said. He waited. "What do we do now?" he asked when Fred declined to fill the silence.

"You made it this far. You tell me."

Harry considered. "We don't know who is up there. It could be late-night tourists. It could be Lauren, alone or with friends. Or it could be park rangers. Which I doubt. Seeing as we have no idea who's up there, and they don't know we're here, we have an advantage. Let's keep it that way. We get out of the car and approach on foot. See what we can see, then go from there. Maybe whoever's up there isn't even near the stone circle. We sneak up on them and then decide what's next."

"What if whoever is up there is not friendly?"

He'd heard his dad discuss this enough to know the answer. "Then we figure out how to get what we want without a fight."

"Work smart, not hard. Brains overcome brawn every time."

"Every time?"

Fred shrugged. "Most of the time. If that fails, run like hell."

Harry turned to his dad. "Run like hell?"

"And don't look back. Took me exactly one good butt-kicking to learn the true value of that advice. You can thank me later for saving you the experience."

Harry laid out a simple plan of attack. He and Fred would approach from either side, taking care to stay well back of the source of that light ahead until they understood who they faced. Scope out the situation, then reconvene near Fred's car. Cell service was nonexistent this far out, so they would be out of touch while reconnoitering. With that rudimentary plan in place, they quietly exited the car and walked toward the dim light. Fred tapped Harry on the shoulder as the ground began to rise beneath their feet. "We'll be visible once we reach the top of this hill," he whispered. "Keep low, keep quiet, and meet me back here in twenty minutes."

Fred Fox turned and disappeared into the darkness to their left. Harry shouldered his pack, ran to the right, stumbled and nearly went flying, then slowed to a quick walk through the waist-high grass, crouching low to keep out of sight and always checking that nothing backlit him. Slick rock stuck out through the dirt and grass in places to make his footing treacherous. A chill wind blew off and on, and though he kept his head down and steered clear of the single road leading to the stone circle, he didn't think it mattered, not with how loudly his heart hammered in his chest and the blood roared in his ears. Anybody up there had to hear the thudding inside him. They'd know he was coming, be ready before he ever—*stop it.*

He came to a halt and shook his head. Shook it hard enough to clear the nonsense away. *Get a grip, Harry. You made it through that cave, the underground chamber and down the well, slipped loose from that iron cage.* Those times had put him on his back foot, forced him to react. Now he was taking the fight to them, to whoever was here. This was his show. *Stop worrying.* He had this.

He pushed everything else aside and focused on getting his backside to the top of the hill without making any noise. The gentle grade of the hillside grew steeper as he moved, with the crest some twenty feet of rise above his head as he moved from the bottom of the slope to the top. From there he could look down on the circle, which stood on a flat piece of ground that overlooked Lough Inchiquin. The top of another giant hill situated across the water, not big enough to be a mountain but plenty high, could be seen even from here. *The water.* That mattered, but how? That question consumed him so completely that he was halfway up the hillside before he saw it. A car several hundred yards to one side, pulled off the narrow road that wound through the park. Pulled off in a perfect spot beside a massive boulder to render it nearly invisible. If it hadn't been for moonlight glinting off the windshield he'd have missed it.

Looks an awful lot like Lauren's car. As did twenty thousand other vehicles in Ireland. It could be anyone's car. The thought stuck in his head as he stared at the car, the dark paint keeping it well hidden under a night sky now leaning toward dawn, with the faintest hint of the coming day on the horizon. Harry crept up the hillside, poked his nose above the top, and looked down at Uragh Stone Circle.

Five stones stood in a ring on the grassy field below. One was easily double the size of the other four, and two of those four defied gravity by standing at forty-five-degree angles, somehow still upright after so many centuries. The big stone must have had a carving on it. One he couldn't see from here, though it had to be there. How else to explain why the two people standing in the circle both stared at that particular stone? A man with a cane, and beside him, a woman with long, curly hair. A woman he knew quite well.

Lauren. She hadn't gone to Cong. She'd come here. He shouldn't be surprised. A scholar like her would uncover the truth, same as he had, but who was the guy with her? Harry peered at him, stared for a long time, and as the darkness above softened and the man began speaking, he realized. The man with Lauren was the same man who had accosted him near the Fal Stone. Harry knew that voice. The guy had a cane now, seemed to lean heavily on one leg when he moved, but it was him. Harry let out a long breath. How in the world had this guy hooked up with Lauren?

The answer hit him right away. *Because they were together before. Lauren was at the Fal Stone.*

Images ran across his mind's eye. He'd only caught a glimpse of the woman he'd trapped inside the chamber. Could it have been Lauren?

The duo had surprised him in the chamber, appearing out of nowhere and shouting to the heavens about him trespassing and asking who he was, making enough of a ruckus that he'd never stopped to consider whether their story held water. All he could come up with when he tried to recall the woman's face was a generic image. Red hair? Brown? Hard to say other than it was dark. It could have been her. He looked at the dark grass and chided himself. *Stop making excuses.* Logic dictated the reason Lauren had found him at Kealkill was that she'd already found him at the Fal Stone. *All things being equal, the simplest explanation is the likeliest one.* Lauren had been at the Fal Stone, along with another man, a man Harry *had* got a good look at. The guy in the chamber resembled the guy here at Uragh Stone Circle.

"Don't forget this," he told himself. Trusting people came with risks. Next time he'd know better.

Lauren and her companion continued to talk while standing in front of the tallest stone. The man did most of the talking, and though Harry couldn't make out most of what he said, the bits he did catch sounded an awful lot like confusion. He caught *Nuada* and *Danu* a few times, references to water, and while Lauren didn't say much, she did point across the shimmering body of water behind her more than once. Her finger indicated the small mountain beyond, though for what reason Harry couldn't say.

The circle sat at the bottom of a small bowl-shaped depression in the land, with the ground on three sides of the circle rising slightly to the level where Harry lay, while the fourth side sloped downward to the lake behind Lauren. She motioned to the small mountain again. She would need to skirt a small body of water if she wanted to get over to the mountain perhaps a half-mile distant. Their flashlights would give Harry a perfect way to track them if they left. He looked in vain for his father across the way, and as he did the hairs on his arm stood up. Why? He checked his watch and found he'd been lying on this hillside for nearly twenty minutes. Time to go.

Harry crept back down from the ridge until he could no longer see Lauren and the man. He stood, turned, and a giant appeared from the shadows.

The giant pointed a gun at Harry's face.

Chapter 13

"Hands up."

The gun barrel hovering inches from his nose looked like the entrance to the Lincoln Tunnel. Harry lifted his hands.

"Turn around." A cloud moved and the slowly falling moon lit the giant's face. The man stood a head taller than Harry, his shoulders roughly as wide as a doorway, and the Irish accent sounded straight out of Dublin. Knuckles the size of walnuts made the gun in his hand seem like a toy. A toy that could still put a hole in people. "Walk to the stones. Don't run or I'll shoot you."

The man spoke without passion, as though he were asking Harry for the time. His eyes were strangely devoid of life. Harry believed every word.

Harry kept his hands up as he walked up and over the hilltop and kept going, grass rustling as he descended toward the stone circle. A warming horizon promised the day's first light when Lauren and the limping man noticed Harry marching down the hill. The glow of Lauren's flashlight revealed utter shock on her face as he walked into the stone's clearing and up to her. The man with the cane studied Harry with something approaching bemusement.

The big man ordered Harry to stop. "I found him up there."

Cane man responded. "Seems you were correct, Maurice."

"Told you I heard a car," Maurice said. He walked up beside Harry, the gun now at his side. "Where'd you park?" he asked Harry.

Harry put his hands down and ignored the big man. He faced Lauren. "You lied about everything."

She opened her mouth with what he hoped would be a protest, but the cane man cut her off. "You should be more careful," he told Harry.

Lauren snapped a reply. "Tom, stop it." She turned to Harry. "I didn't lie about everything."

"Are you a student?" he asked. No response. "Didn't think so. You knew I'd be up there. You were at the Fal Stone. Both of you were."

"You should have listened to us," Tom said. "This isn't a journey you want to take. It's meant for others."

"It's meant for the person who found the first tablet," Harry said. "That's me."

Tom aimed his cane at Harry's pack. "Is the tablet in there?" Harry's frown gave the answer. "Give me the pack," Tom said.

One look at big Maurice told Harry there were times to resist, and times to obey. This was the latter. He shrugged his pack off and handed it to Tom. "They're both in there. The one from the cave and the one from the Fal Stone."

"Appreciate you bringing them," Tom said as he opened the pack and confirmed what Harry said. "Finally. The tablets are back where they belong." He took the tablets and tossed the pack back to Harry.

"Belong?" Harry asked. "What makes you think these are yours?"

Tom lifted his eyebrows. "You really don't know, do you? Lauren said you were smart." He shook his head. "Apparently she was wrong."

Harry looked at Lauren, who had her eyes on the ground. "We'll see about that," Harry said.

Lauren looked up. "How did you get here?" she asked.

"I drove."

"No. How did you know to come here, to this circle?"

Harry shrugged. "Same way you did. I found a connection between a stone circle and Nuada's arm." He looked at the tall stone for the first time, and Lauren aimed her light at it. "Wasn't hard once I had cell service."

"Which we do not have here." Tom checked his phone again, briefly, and an instant later his head shot back up and he stared at Harry. "Lauren," he said, his eyes on Harry. "Tell me again how you evaded this man at Kealkill."

"I took his car keys." She said it softly. "He couldn't go anywhere without them."

"It's well over an hour from Kealkill to here," Tom said. "Maurice heard you arrive some time ago." Tom pointed his cane at Harry. "How did you get here so fast with no car keys?"

A moment's hesitation was all he needed. "I had a spare in my pack."

Tom still watched him. "Lauren, tell me what you heard when you went to your car while he was on the phone."

Lauren's face hardened. "He took a call, wouldn't tell me who it was. That was my chance. I took his keys with me to my car and heard the alert beeping."

"The alert saying no key was detected," Tom said. "Did it stop when he came back to the car?" Lauren said it did not. "Which means you don't have a spare," Tom said. "I think you had help. Someone came to get you. That's the only way you could get here so quickly." Tom snapped his fingers. "Maurice, I'm going to ask Harry a question. If he lies to me again, shoot him."

Maurice aimed his pistol at Harry's chest. Tom's voice rang loud and clear when he spoke. "Did you come here alone?" he asked. "Three seconds." A beat passed during which Tom looked in every direction. "Three seconds or you get a bullet in the leg. Did you come alone?"

"It's just me," Harry said, keeping his hands down. *Don't come out, Dad. They won't shoot me.*

"One."

Harry had no idea if he was right. "I'm here alone," he said.

"Two."

Harry tensed. Tom had a cane. Maybe he could get close to the guy fast enough that Maurice wouldn't shoot for fear of hitting Tom. Maurice set his feet. No doubt he would shoot.

Tom opened his mouth. "Thr—"

"Wait!"

Fred Fox leapt above the ridgeline. "Don't shoot. He came with me." He stood outlined against the warming skyline as Tom aimed his light at the noise.

Maurice groaned at the missed opportunity. "Don't lie to me again," Tom said to Harry. He turned to Fred and raised his voice. "Wise decision. Come down here."

Fred ambled down the hillside in no particular hurry. Tom's flashlight beam followed him the entire way until Fred reached the clearing and Tom ordered him to stop. "Who are you?" Tom asked.

"Name's Fred."

"Why are you here?"

"To find the end of a mythical Irish path."

"An honest man," Tom said. "How refreshing. What do you know?"

"That we're in the right place," Fred replied.

"How do you know that?"

"You're here." Fred pointed at one of the tablets Tom held. "Which tells me you reached the same conclusion we did as to what that tablet means. Two people getting the same answer is a good sign the answer is correct."

"And what did you plan to do here?" Tom asked.

"See what you found and then go from there."

"Are you armed?" Fred said he was not. "Nothing personal," Tom said. "But I have to check. Come over here and let my associate verify you're telling the truth."

Tom inclined his head toward Maurice, and only after Fred walked over and let Maurice check for weapons did Tom speak again. "It seems we are all on the same path," Tom said. "Who else knows you are here?"

"Friends back home," Fred said.

"You mean Vincent Morello."

"I see you're well informed."

"You will tell your boss I hold no ill will toward him," Tom said. "I have the utmost respect for him. However, this is an Irish matter, not an Italian one. We should respect each other's territory equally."

"I'm sure he feels the same way," Fred said. "Unless you shoot one of us. That would change things."

"Then don't give me a reason to shoot you."

"Wasn't planning on it."

Harry had heard enough. "Who are you guys?" he blurted out with heat in his words. "You send some spy to trick me into telling her what I know about the stones so you two can finally figure this out, and now you want to shoot us."

Lauren did not take kindly to his words. "We didn't need you," she fired back. "You were lucky. That's it. I would have unraveled the mystery if I had the first tablet."

"But you didn't," Harry said. "I did. Don't make it seem like luck. The only reason you're here is because of me."

"Perhaps we shouldn't antagonize the people with guns," Fred said evenly. "What matters is nobody gets hurt." He looked at Tom. "That's all I care about. Understood?" Tom made a noncommittal gesture. "I'll take that as a yes," Fred said before turning to Harry. "Forget it, Harry. None of this matters. All I want is to get out of here alive."

"It matters a great deal," Lauren said. "You Americans have no idea."

Fred raised an eyebrow. "Why does it matter?"

"Because control of our land was stolen," Lauren said. "Time and again. This path will prove it. It's how we can regain control of our destiny. Of Ireland's destiny."

Harry started putting the puzzle pieces together. "That's why you kept going on about the government," he said. "About people sitting on stolen seats." He put a hand out to indicate Tom. "Do you think he's the real president of Ireland or something? That doesn't make any sense. Presidents are elected."

"Our republic rests on authority from a false parliament." Tom's words would have lit the night sky if the sun weren't already about to rise. "A republic built on a constitution that does not represent the people."

"You prefer a monarchy?" Fred asked lightly. "The men and women who fought Great Britain a century ago may disagree."

"Don't lecture me on our history," Tom said. "You have no idea of the truth."

"Then please, enlighten me."

Lauren jumped in before Tom could reply. "The world has no idea of the truth—that our fellow Irish are being denied appropriate representation."

"You have a representative democracy," Fred said. "The parliament is elected by the people."

"The parliament sits on stolen seats," Lauren retorted. "The legitimacy of all Irish leaders has been incomplete for two thousand years. Ever since the Romans tried to conquer our island. Tried and failed."

"Enough," Tom said, turning to glare at her.

"No." Harry's interest was piqued. "I want to know why you're here."

Lauren hesitated only a moment before going on. "To prove what we believe is true."

"Prove?" Harry asked. "You mean you don't know if it's even true?"

"It's true." Her words brooked no dissent. "You proved it. Our ancestors hid four items from the Romans so they couldn't conquer Ireland by stealing our way of life. The Romans only managed to steal our beliefs, but they could never claim legitimacy by taking the holy objects."

"The Tuatha Dé Danann," Harry said. "Their sacred relics."

"The first of which is the Fal Stone," Lauren said. "Hidden in plain sight. You understood their plan without me telling you."

Harry turned to his father. "She's talking about Midsummer."

"Rome wanted to reappropriate it," Fred said. "Standard procedure for them. Mainly because it worked."

"The Romans repurposed the Irish pagan festival of Midsummer into their festival honoring the goddess Fortuna," Harry said. "A celebration of the summer, of crop harvests and long, warm days. A celebration of the earth's bounty."

"Which the Christians then stole for their purposes," Lauren said. "The Feast of Saint John, when fires are lit on the longest day of the year to celebrate the summer solstice."

Fred cleared his throat. "Which should be halfway between the annual celebration of Jesus' birth. However, Saint John is honored on the twenty-fourth of June, not the twenty-fifth."

"Which is a day earlier than it should be," Lauren said. "You do know your history," she said with grudging admiration. "Had the Christians truly created their feast day on their own, instead of stealing it, the feast would be on the twenty-fifth. It's a day early because of how the Romans counted days in a month."

Fred smiled as though she were an astute pupil. "Romans counted backwards from the first day of the succeeding month. Not forward from the first day of the current month. That put the feast a day before the mathematically correct midpoint between Christmases."

"More evidence of our true leaders being usurped," Lauren said.

"Many kings were toppled from their throne by force," Fred said.

"But how many are determined enough to wait two thousand years before reclaiming their throne?" she replied.

"Is that your goal?" Fred asked.

Tom finally spoke. "No. We merely want representation. A seat for the"—a beat passed—"*person* who has Ireland's best interests at heart. Not the corrupt elected officials owned by donors. A person whose sole objective is to consider the interests of every Irish citizen, not only those with money."

"A man of the people," Fred said.

"You have no understanding of what we desire," Tom said. "You are an American. An interloper on our island."

"Does that make me your enemy?"

"It makes you someone I cannot trust. I understand you are a professional. You have ties to men who know how to guard their trust. It's nothing personal."

"I'll remember that when you shoot me."

"Perhaps I will," Tom said. "Perhaps not." He casually removed a pistol from inside his coat and waved it. "Enough of your questions. We have one for you. What do you believe this symbol represents?" Now his gun indicated the tallest stone in the circle. "You made it this far," he said, turning to Harry. "What would you do next?"

Fred looked ready to speak, but Harry jumped in. "I got this one, Dad." Harry pointed at the engraving on the tall stone. "That's—"

"*Dad?*" Lauren's eyes went wide. "This man is your father?"

"Yeah," Harry said. "So what?"

"Why is your father here?"

"Because he's good at this sort of thing," Harry said. "You might have learned that if you hadn't stolen my tablet and left me at Kealkill."

"I left you because you didn't trust me," she fired back. "You left the car to make a phone call and wouldn't tell me who it was."

"I was calling my *dad*."

Lauren's eyes widened. "What sort of relic hunter calls their father for advice?"

"He's experienced in this sort of thing."

"It's the truth," Tom said. "Think, Lauren. Harry Fox has ties to the Morello crime family. He isn't part of it. He doesn't work for them, but he's tied to them." Tom pointed the hand without a gun at Fred. "My intelligence didn't specify how, but I am sure it's because of this man. His father must work for Vincent Morello."

"We have a business relationship," Fred said. "Which is not important. Unless you think about shooting us. Then you might want to think about what could happen to you."

"This isn't America," Tom said. "And these loughs are very deep. Do as we say and everything will be fine."

Harry spotted an angle he didn't like. "You're not worried we'll tell anyone about your little clan of royalists?"

"Who would believe you?" Tom asked. "It works because it is so easily dismissed. And if you told anyone I would find out. You'd be my enemy. Maurice's enemy. Do you want that?"

Harry looked at the big man. "I do not."

"Good. Now, the stone. What do you make of that carving?"

Harry and the others turned to look. A well-muscled arm graced the center of the tallest stone, the carving depicting it so Harry looked at what he would term the outside section of the arm. A rounded shoulder, a thick bicep and forearm, with the hand partly obscured by a shield that had been sliced in half.

"It's a right arm," Harry said. "Cut off at the shoulder and holding what looks like half a shield."

"Which is how the myth describes Nuada's wound," Lauren said. "His right arm was severed at the shoulder, and the blow also cut away a portion of his shield."

"Then we're looking at the right arm." A pause. No laughter. "Anyway," Harry continued. "You can see part of his hand where the shield was cut away. Lucky for Nuada they didn't slice his fingers off too."

"That's not part of the myth," Lauren said. "At least no version I ever read."

Harry looked at Tom and Maurice in turn. "What about you guys? Ever hear a version where his fingers are cut off?"

"I've never read anything about his fingers," Tom said. "Though in all fairness, I would lean on Lauren for this information."

"No versions I know of discuss his hands," Lauren said. "The only injury reference is loss of the right arm."

Harry looked at Fred. Fred raised an eyebrow. "Interesting."

"We thought so as well," Lauren said.

Harry took a step toward the stone. "You know what catches my eye?" he asked. "This."

What had once been a circular shield was sliced in half, not in a direct line across the entire diameter but in a curving line, creating a crescent moon shape that revealed Nuada's knuckles and fingers. One finger was extended, pointing toward the edge of the stone. Or, perhaps, elsewhere. "Only one finger points outward," Harry said. "That can't be accidental."

"My thought as well," Lauren said. She moved past him, her arm brushing his, and she kept moving until she could reach out and touch the stone. "I checked the edge of the stone. There is no evidence of a hidden compartment or chamber. The stone is solid. I can't find anything to suggest otherwise."

Harry was only half-listening. He looked to his father, then back to the stone, before his gaze returned to Fred. His dad lifted an eyebrow as if to say *What do you think?* That was all the encouragement he needed.

"The message on the tablet had three lines," Harry said. "Three focal points. Nuada, Danu and Manann. Nuada's right here." He pointed to the tallest stone. "What about Danu and Manann? Danu is the sun god, and Manann is tied to the water. What's Nuada's finger pointing to?"

"The lough," Lauren said. "You think we need to search the lough? It's massive, and also likely quite deep." She frowned. "It could be near where the sunlight hits. The light could point to a stone marker either in the grass or in shallow water."

Red turning burnt orange tinged the skyline now. Harry narrowed his eyes. "Water makes sense. But do you really think your ancestors would have buried anything underwater? They didn't have scuba gear back then." He looked at the lightening sky as he spoke, and for some reason he couldn't quite articulate, he knew he was on the right path, so close to the truth he could nearly see it. All he needed to do was wait. "Look toward the sun. Not at the water. Toward the sun."

It didn't take long. One moment the night held on, and before Harry realized it had happened, the sun appeared on the horizon. He kept one hand over his eyes to shield them from the light. He waited. Nobody could see, but he was grinning. "I knew it."

"What did you say?" Lauren asked.

"I know where Nuada is pointing. Look at the mountain across the lake. There's a valley halfway up. A small portion of the mountain that looks like it was cut out. See it?"

It took Lauren a moment. "The two sides of the valley are framing the sun," she said. "That's exactly where the sun came up. Right beside the waterfall."

A waterfall Harry had only noticed minutes ago. "Go to that waterfall," Harry said. "And you'll find what you seek."

Chapter 14

Uragh Circle, County Kerry

Nobody argued with Harry about trekking to the valley. After Tom let Harry stow the tablets in his pack for safekeeping, it took the better part of an hour to hike around the lake and get to the tree line on the far shore, a tree line that appeared far thicker from a distance than it turned out to be up close. The tall trees did a wonderful job of blocking the sunlight, though under the canopy the trunks were spread out far enough that their group could walk in a ragged line with little trouble and no fear of losing each other. Fred Fox had a compass, because of course he did, and it led them on a direct route to the bottom of the valley below the waterfall Harry believed held the secret to Nuada's pointing finger.

They descended into the valley in short order, following the quickly moving stream that cascaded down the mountainside in fits and spurts, until one last leg-burning climb up a much steeper hillside brought them to a patch of level ground at the upper end of the small valley. The waterfall tumbled from some thirty feet above, splashing into a pool Harry had no intention of entering, and when he looked back across the edge of the lake toward the stone circle, he knew they had arrived.

"This is where the sun came over the mountainside," Harry said. "I'm certain of it."

Maurice had kept behind everyone as they trekked, stumping along wordlessly, the pistol never leaving his hand. Tom's gun had gone back into his coat. Now, he gritted his teeth, leaned against a tree and moved his ankle back and forth. "I'd shoot you if you weren't so useful," he told Harry.

Harry ignored him. Sheer rock surrounded them to either side, so steep only mountain goats could hope to scale it, while the trees ended a few feet behind them. "You'd never know this open spot existed unless you stumbled across it," Harry said. "It looked like a thick forest from the stone circle."

"A good place to hide something," Lauren said. "One problem. What do we do now?"

Fred Fox had remained mostly silent until now. "I have an idea," he said. "Think about how you got here."

Harry realized a lesson when it was foisted upon him. "You don't mean walking through the forest."

"I mean the messages and clues you followed. What did the Irish pagans write on? Stone tablets. Why? So their messages would last. They wouldn't have suspected the messages would need to last for two thousand years, but they did. What would they do up here to point you in the correct direction?"

Lauren proved an adept student. "We need to check the cliffside," she said. "And the ground. There could be a message carved into the mountain or the earth."

"I'd start with the mountainside," Fred suggested. "Near the waterfall."

"Which would give added meaning to the message about Manann," Harry said. "Good call."

Fred lifted a shoulder. *All in a day's work.*

Harry noted Tom didn't move to help, and Maurice stayed back, the gun still in hand. Harry and Lauren stood shoulder to shoulder at the edge of the pool. Its icy spray reached up to his bare skin, setting it alight with cold pinpricks. "There's a ton of moss and growth on the mountainside," Harry said. "It's basically vertical all the way up. Like a giant wall."

"Do you have a knife?" Lauren asked. Harry said he did not. "Neither do I. Come on." She grabbed his arm and pulled him after her. "Rip the vines and moss off with your hands," she said, then called over a shoulder. "Come on, Fred. We need another pair of hands."

Fred Fox didn't have to be asked twice. Harry took one side, Fred the other, and Lauren stayed between them. Wet leaves, green moss and chunks of dirt flew as they worked. Early morning sunlight trickled down the mountainside as stone hidden for untold years finally came into view. Gray stone, craggy and entirely unremarkable; nothing to suggest Harry's interpretation of the ancient message was correct. He cut his finger on a sharp outcropping, swore, and Lauren jumped back from the wall.

"Look at this." She pointed at the stone she had been clearing. "It looks like writing."

Harry and Fred surrounded her in an instant, both reaching out to touch the unnaturally straight line on the cliffside. "It's weathered," Fred said. "And you're right. It could be a letter. A letter that has been here a long time."

Harry ripped more dirt away. "Here's another letter," he said. "A *U* and an *S*." The gouges were worn by rain and time, so faded they could have been natural markings, but two of them beside each other and on the same level? No chance this was natural. He feverishly pulled debris away to reveal the truth. "Whoa." Harry stepped back. "I was right."

Three letters had materialized on the cliff in front of him. A name. "*Use*," Harry said. "I knew I was right."

Fred and Lauren were still busy clearing the wall. Harry returned to his own work, and moments later he stepped back, grime beneath his nails and on his forehead, now able to read a message hidden for centuries. Three words inscribed in a single line on the mountainside. "*Use Lugh's Power*," Harry said. He turned to Lauren. "Who is Lugh?"

"A warrior and a king," she said. "One of the Tuatha, a god of justice and war."

"And his power?"

"I'm not sure," she said.

"I know how to find out," Fred told them. He stepped to Harry's portion of the wall and began pulling debris away. Not on the same level as the three words they had revealed, but below them.

"What are you doing?" Lauren asked.

"Finding the answer," Fred said. "I'll find it faster if you two help. Clear the dirt off this rock."

Seconds after they jumped in to help, the answer arrived. "Look at this," Fred said. "Another line carved into the stone." He pulled another chunk of debris loose. "Never mind. This isn't a line."

"It's a face." Lauren elbowed Fred aside and clawed at the wall in front of her. "It's Lugh! I'm sure of it. The hair is unmistakable."

Harry saw a big man with curled hair and a great cloak around his shoulders. One arm was at his side and held a spear. The other was lifted so the palm faced Harry, as though Lugh was waving at him. "Is that spear his power?" Harry asked. "You said he had long arms. Those aren't that long."

"He is known for use of a spear," Lauren said as she brushed the last bit of debris away. "As to the long arms, the phrase *long arm* is interchangeable with *long hand*. I suspect it's a reference to his ability with a spear."

"How can we use his spear?" Harry leaned toward the wall and touched the weathered lines. "It's a carving of a line with a triangle on the end. We can't use it for anything."

A hand touching his shoulder made Harry jump. Fred nudged him gently aside, never looking at Harry, only at the wall. "Not all is as it seems," Fred said. A gentle breeze rustled the trees. A bird cried out in the woods. Fred stepped closer to the wall. "You say this Lugh god was referred to as 'long hand'?" Lauren said this was correct. "Which ties to his prowess with a spear?"

"He was said to be unstoppable in battle with the spear."

"I wonder." Fred rubbed his chin. "The ancient Irish have proven resourceful with their mythology so far. I wonder if they're at it again."

Harry knew better than to ask questions when his dad got that look on this face. Lines on his forehead, eyes slightly narrowed, looking at something only he could see. Lauren opened her mouth as though to speak. Harry waved her into silence. The carving of Lugh had been detailed at one point a long time ago, though now most of the lines were faded and the image was more shadow than sharp, but it had grabbed his dad's attention and wouldn't let go. What had done it?

Fred reached out for Lugh's hand. The palm faced Fred, and his dad put his hand on the god's palm, resting it there, standing still. He leaned closer to the stone, so close his nose nearly touched the carved lines. Fred stayed there, studying the wall, looking at it for so long without moving that Harry decided he'd seen enough and needed to know what in the world had Fred's eye. Stand here long enough, he reasoned, and the two men with guns might get impatient.

"Stand back." Fred's words came out of nowhere. Harry asked why. "I have an idea," was all his dad said. Harry shrugged and stepped back,

Lauren following suit. Only after they were clear did Fred lean against the stone wall with one hand on Lugh's palm, leaning normally at first before putting his other hand on top of the first one and pushing. His feet dug into the dirt, the muscles on his arms swelled, and he gritted his teeth. Fred pushed on the wall with everything he had, and as he stood nearly a head taller than his son, Fred had a lot to push with.

The wall cracked. Dirt erupted as Lugh's palm slid into the sheer stone. Fred kept pushing until his arms disappeared halfway to the elbows. That's when the wall shook.

The ground rumbled, dirt fell from far above, and as Harry's mouth fell open, a hole appeared in the side of the mountain. A section of the wall fell inward on invisible hinges to reveal a gaping maw of darkness ahead. A hole big enough to drive a pickup truck through.

Harry didn't realize the rumbling had stopped until his dad spoke. "I thought that might work." Fred dusted his hands off and turned to Harry. "You have a flashlight I can borrow?"

Harry pulled a light from his pack and handed it to his dad, keeping one for himself as well. They both turned toward the new opening.

"Wait." Tom hobbled closer to them. "Do not go inside."

Fred glanced at Harry with a look that said *I'll handle this.* "No problem," Fred said. He put the flashlight down and stepped back. "It's all yours."

Harry was busy trying to figure out why his dad would yield so easily when Tom spoke again. "Maurice, you go first. Tell me what you see inside."

The big man told Tom to get his pistol out and herded Harry and Fred together, making them stand close to Tom, but not so close they could rush the injured man and get his gun. Only then did Maurice put his pistol away and take out a flashlight of his own. The waterfall rumbled as every person in front of the newly opened tunnel edged closer, their lights aimed at the darkness, eyes narrowed to see anything they could. Maurice stopped on the threshold and leaned forward, peering into the darkness.

"There's writing on the wall." His light went to the left tunnel wall. Lauren darted closer to see it. Harry and Fred followed suit, stopping short of Maurice, but standing close enough that they could see. "I can't read it," Maurice said.

Harry could. "*Only after opening Danu's knowledge will you recover the treasure.*" He glanced at Fred. "Sound right?" Harry asked. Fred said it did.

"That's the correct translation," Lauren said to the group. She stood beside Maurice on the threshold, closer than Harry and Fred. "There are carvings in the wall beneath the message." A pause. "And three notches."

Fred spoke up. "Notches?"

"Small holes," Lauren said. "Come here—you can see them."

"That is close enough," Tom said. "Stay back. We can handle this."

Another shrug from Fred, as though the message didn't much interest him. Why wasn't his dad pushing to get closer? Harry didn't know why, but Fred didn't do anything without a good reason, so he kept his mouth shut and stayed back with his dad. "Describe the carvings," Harry said.

Lauren spoke with a scholar's detachment. "I see three rectangles. The shorter sides are on the top and bottom, the longer sides on the right and left. All are level with each other, and are approximately the size of a shoebox. They are evenly spaced beneath the Latin letters. Each rectangle is bisected by a horizontal, jagged line resembling a bolt of lightning."

"Any writing on the rectangles?" Harry asked.

"None. The only other marks on the wall are the notches. One is directly below each rectangle."

"Turn around." Maurice's words echoed off the stone walls. "Look at this."

He pointed at the right side of the tunnel. Only when their combined flashlight beams aimed that way did Harry notice it. A life-sized statue of Lugh faced the carved rectangles and Latin message. "Looks like he means business with that spear," Harry said. The statue had one arm upraised, holding a spear aloft as though ready to hurl it through the far wall. "What's Danu's knowledge?" he asked Lauren. "I don't remember reading anything about that."

"Danu is the goddess of wisdom," Lauren said. "A number of myth sources indicate Danu gifted knowledge to the Tuatha gods. All knowledge."

"Which could mean anything," Harry said. "Not helpful."

"It is if you know how to interpret the words," Fred said. "Look at it through the lens of this search. The ancient Irish had a purpose: to hide their treasures from the Romans. Any messages they left must serve this goal in some way."

Maurice had turned away from the conversation nearly as soon as it began. He had been quiet, looking into the tunnel. Until now. "There's a bridge up there," he said. The big man took a long step into the tunnel. "Looks narrow." Another step. "I can't see it with all these cobwebs." Maurice reached out and waved his hand through the string of webs crisscrossing the tunnel from floor to ceiling. "Dumb webs," he said as more thick strands came tumbling down.

"I wouldn't do that," Fred said. "We don't understand the message yet."

Maurice waved a dismissive hand covered in web. "Figure it out. I bet that bridge leads to the treasure." He took another step. "I can see—"

His words were cut off as he tripped, arms wheeling as he stumbled forward and tried to catch his balance. A familiar noise filled Harry's ears. *Twang.* The noise of a guitar string being plucked. Or a hidden wire.

"Wait!" Harry lunged forward.

Maurice turned at the shout just as the tunnel walls on each side of him exploded. Spears shot from either wall with a deadly hissing sound, fired from all angles to envelop the tunnel in a rain of deadly wood and iron. They slammed into their opposite walls, bounced off the ground and clattered out of the tunnel. Harry twisted aside as one spear as tall as him flew between his arm and chest before burying itself in a tree trunk. The wooden shaft quivered and the metal tip stuck fast.

"Maurice!"

Tom O'Connor raced into the cave, injured ankle and all. Only Fred Fox darting out to grab him stopped Tom from reaching Maurice's body. A body with two spears in it. They had penetrated clean through Maurice's torso, the iron points and shafts protruding from his now lifeless form.

"Stay back," Fred shouted at Tom. "You don't know what else is in there."

Tom snarled and tried to throw Fred off without success. Only when he pointed the pistol in Fred's direction did Fred let him go. Tom took one step toward the cave mouth and stopped. He stared at his friend's body, his mouth hanging open, his shoulders drooping as he said a single word. "Maurice."

"There was a tripwire in the cobwebs," Harry said. "I heard it break." He turned to Lauren. "The same type of wire we tripped in the well." Lauren confirmed she heard it too "Don't go in there until we know what we're up against," Harry said to the group.

"You killed my friend." Tom still hadn't turned away from Maurice's corpse. "You killed him."

Lauren put a hand on Tom's shoulder. "No one killed him, Tom. It was a trap left by our ancestors. To protect their treasures."

"No." Tom's voice carried a hard finality. "No."

Harry flinched when Tom turned to him. The man's eyes promised a fury would be unleashed. Harry didn't have to guess upon whom.

The pistol barrel pointed at Harry's chest. "You knew."

"Knew what?" Harry was halfway to putting his hands up before stopping himself. "He barged in there on his own," Harry said. "I had no idea."

"Put the gun down." Fred said it gently. "Be reasonable. Nobody knew what would happen."

"The time for reason has passed." Tom turned the gun on Fred. "It's time to complete the mission. Maurice died for this. No other Irishman will."

Fred lifted an eyebrow, not his hands. "You believe shooting me will help?"

"Only if necessary." Tom looked at Harry. "Go with Lauren. It seems you have some horrid luck or skill, I don't know which, but you have survived so far. You are responsible for this." Here he indicated the corpse. "Which makes you responsible for making his death not be in vain. Help Lauren recover the treasures."

Harry wasn't buying it. "Those treasures may be long gone. Even if they're not, you have no clue what they are."

"I know exactly what they are."

The man had conviction, Harry would give him that. "Fine," Harry said. "Say there's something in there. And say we get it. How do I know you won't shoot us after that?"

Tom ignored the question. "Help her, or I shoot your father in the leg."

"How considerate," Fred said.

"Enough," Tom said. "Into the cave. Find the treasures." His voice grew a bit softer. "Find our destiny."

Harry turned to Lauren. If she was conflicted about the threat of bodily harm and her supposed destiny, she didn't show it. In fact, she didn't even look his way as they walked side by side into the cave, giving the corpse a wide berth and stopping short of a spear sticking out of the ground. Harry aimed his flashlight deeper into the cave. "Two more statues of Lugh," he said as his light moved from one to the other. "One on each side." The statues were staggered, with the closest on their left and the farthest to their right.

"The statues offer full coverage of the tunnel," Lauren said. "Assuming they are armed with spears or other weapons like the first one, there's no way to the bridge that doesn't pass those statues."

"Which tells me there's a way to deactivate them," Harry said. "The Irish wanted their treasure to be recovered. They didn't make it impossible."

"Merely deadly," Lauren said. "I am open to suggestions on how to reach that bridge."

Harry peered into the distance for some time. The bridge wasn't exactly a bridge, he realized. More of a narrow stone walkway running down the center of the cave, with what appeared to be vast holes on either side. A *very* narrow walkway. He frowned. A problem for later. "Your answer is over there." He pointed back to the three rectangles and the Latin words. "Understand the meaning, and you'll find the answer."

"What do three broken rectangles have to do with the treasure of the Tuatha?"

Harry started. "Broken? Why do you say that?"

Lauren moved her finger in a zig-zag pattern. "Those irregular lines in the middle make the rectangles appear broken. To me, at least. I'm not certain."

Harry snapped his fingers. "You *should* be certain. Darn, I never saw it. You're right."

"What are you talking about?"

He walked to the carvings and took his pack off, setting it on the ground. "The answer has been in front of us this whole time. I know what these carvings are." He removed one of the tablets from the pack. "These. The carvings are tablets. And they're telling us what to do."

Chapter 15

County Kerry

"I found three tablets, remember."

Harry aimed the single stone tablet in his hand at the wall. "And there are three rectangles on the wall. Each rectangle represents a tablet. And that lightning bolt in the middle of each one? Those are instructions."

Harry pulled the three tablets he'd recovered on this adventure from his pack, handing two of them to Lauren. "You're not going to like this," he told Tom. "Don't shoot."

Before Tom knew what happened, Harry had lifted the tablet over his head with both hands and smashed it on a small outcropping in the wall. Rock dust flew, the tablet broke in two, and as Tom was shouting and pointing his pistol at Harry the answer came out. "Look!" Harry pointed at the ground. "I told you."

An iron key lay on the cave floor. "The tablets are more than messages," Harry said. "They're containers. That's what the wall is telling us. Open the containers and retrieve each key."

Lauren's mouth moved more quickly than the words that came out. "But," she sputtered, "how did you know it had a key inside?"

"I didn't," Harry admitted. "That part was a guess. Those three holes beneath each rectangle look like keyholes, and when you said the rectangles were *broken*, I connected the dots. Danu's knowledge is the path, the clues to tell us how to get here. The knowledge is on the tablets. Break the tablets, get the keys, and we can unlock the path ahead."

Lauren handed a second tablet to Harry and raised the third one. They both lifted them at the same time, smashed them down, and when the dust cleared two more iron keys lay on the ground. Harry scooped them up. "They're long," he said. "Nearly a foot, and they're thick. Strong enough to slide into these holes and turn whatever locks are inside."

Lauren took one key, Harry the other two. They inserted all three at the same time, counted down, then twisted simultaneously. Iron grated on rock and Harry gritted his teeth as he forced both of his keys to turn. Lauren used both hands to move hers. All three keys twisted in half-circles with difficulty before lodging in their respective stone locks, each halfway through a full turn.

The wall rumbled. Harry and Lauren jumped back as the sound of ancient gears turning reverberated behind the stone walls for several long seconds, the noise vibrating his teeth and echoing the length of the tunnel. Then, as quickly as it had started, the noises stopped. Nothing else happened. Lauren turned to Harry. "Do you think we deactivated the traps?"

"Only one way to find out."

He glanced back at his father. Fred pumped his fist and nodded. Harry gulped. *I hope this works.*

A shrieking noise of tortured stone nearly sent him out of his skin. A section of tunnel wall below the keyholes had fallen loose and landed on the floor. Harry went to it, bending down and peering inside. "Gold."

That got Tom's attention. "Where?"

"In here." Harry removed a rock roughly the size of a baseball. "This rock is solid gold."

Lauren darted to his side. "How do you know?" Instead of answering he handed it to her. She grunted. "My goodness, this is heavy. You're correct. It must be solid gold."

"Bring it to me," Tom said.

"I will," Harry said. "Later. The Irish didn't leave it here for fun. I bet this golden rock has a purpose." He pointed ahead. "In there."

Lauren backed him up and Tom reluctantly agreed. Harry put the oversized rock in a pocket, grateful he had a belt on to keep his pants up. He strode deeper into the tunnel with a confidence he didn't feel, coming right up to a set of cobwebs that told him the spiders had found something helpful on which to string their webs, something like a long piece of ancient metallic wire. He sucked in a breath and kept walking. The webs resisted more than webs should. He pushed on, and a trio of rapid *twang* noises rang out when the webs gave way.

Harry froze. No spears flew. No further noises sounded. The tunnel did not attack.

A long breath he didn't realize he'd been holding came out. "Nothing to it," he told himself. The next cobweb wall only made his chest seize up for an instant before he pushed through the hidden wires without result once more. He stopped, ripping sheets of sticky, dusty cobweb off himself before turning to call over his shoulder. "I'm through."

His father called back. "What do you see?"

"A stone walkway. Narrow, maybe a foot wide at best. There are deep pits on either side."

"How deep?"

Harry leaned over to look, shining his light down. "Deep. Thirty feet at least. There's water at the bottom of them."

"Don't fall in," Fred offered helpfully. "No telling what's under the water."

Thanks, Dad. "I'll keep that in mind." He waved at Lauren. "You coming?"

She followed his dusty footsteps until she stood at his side. "This walkway is a foot wide all the way down." Her flashlight revealed she spoke the truth. "Do you think it will hold us?"

He offered a now-familiar and still frightening reply. "Only one way to find out."

The idea that treasure hunters who lived a long time wouldn't say that came to his mind. He threw it out. Treasures were like girls. You didn't get them by staying on the sidelines. It took action. "I'll go across first," he said. "Then wait for you. I bet you want to be there when I finally see what all this is about."

"All what?" He put a finger under her flashlight and lifted it. The light went from the narrow column to what lay across from them, at the far end of the path. "You're right," Lauren said, awe in her voice. "I do."

A flat ledge lay at the far end of the walkway. A ledge perhaps twenty feet deep, as wide as the cave, with a sheer stone wall behind it. A ledge with three stone pedestals. Each pedestal had an object atop it. Three objects Harry recognized. "Those are the treasures of the Tuatha Dé Danann," Harry said.

A cauldron on the pedestal to the left. A spear on the one to the right. And in the center, a sword in a belted scabbard looped over the pedestal.

"They are," Lauren confirmed. She waited. He didn't move. "Do you want me to go first?" she asked.

"I want you to tell me the truth." He took his gaze off the treasures. "Have you really been searching for these for two thousand years so you can have some ancient king take control of Ireland?"

Lauren appeared to consider several responses, stopping and starting, but never quite saying anything. "The short answer is yes," she finally said. A drop of water fell from the ceiling and landed on her forehead. She wiped it away. "The longer answer is that we started with that goal two thousand years ago. It has since evolved. I'll explain when we're back outside."

"You'll explain now. Your boss threatened to shoot my dad. I want to know who I'm dealing with."

Lines creased her forehead. "You want to do this now?" Harry said he did, and he wasn't taking no for an answer. "Fine." Lauren crossed her arms. "According to legend, our group formed shortly after the treasures went missing. Its original purpose was to find the treasures and restore them to the rightful king."

Harry knew this story. "A king who would wield the Spear of Lugh, which rendered him undefeatable in battle. A king who would also carry the Sword of Nuada, which defeated every man who stood against it. A king who would welcome all guests with the Cauldron of Dagda, so they never went away unsatisfied. And a king who," he said with a wry smile, "would sit on the Stone of Fal and have it cry out beneath him to show he is the one true Irish king. Did I get that right?"

"Do not mock our beliefs," she said. "But yes, that is correct." She pointed across the chasm and her voice rose. "Here is proof. For two thousand years we did not know if what we searched for even existed. The knowledge was lost. The certainty faded. Yet generation after generation continued the search." Now she spoke softly. "It was all true. Every word."

"Hard to argue with you," he said. "How did you get caught up in this? Family tradition?"

"Something like that," she said. "The first-born of every generation in my family served our cause. Today we're called the Irish Heritage Society. We've had many names over the centuries, but only one purpose."

"To find these treasures and give them to the one true king," Harry said. "One problem with all that." He pointed at the far ledge. "You have the treasures. Where's the king?"

Her mouth became a hard line. "I have not been given that information. The identity of the one true king is known only by our leader."

"Not very safe," Harry said. "What if they die?"

"The truth is written in our secret archives," Lauren said. "Should the leader die, another is allowed to access the information. That is all I know."

"Tom's the leader?" Harry asked as the realization hit him. Lauren said he was. "I was afraid of that."

"Why are you afraid?"

"He's too serious about all this," Harry said. "The kind of guy who kills to keep secrets."

"He won't shoot your father."

"You sure about that?" The look on her face told him all he needed to know. "Thought not," Harry said. "I'll tell you this, and if you cross me, I'll throw you into that pit."

"You wouldn't."

"Try me." Harry lowered his voice lest the echoes betray him back at the entrance. "If he tries anything, I'll toss your precious relics in the lake. After I cut his arm off with the sword. You tell him that when we get out of here. Understood?"

"Nothing will happen," Lauren said. "I know Tom. Trust me."

Harry would do no such thing. "Come on," he said. "Let's get this over with."

The heat boiling inside him over Tom threatening his dad doused any enthusiasm he may have felt. Yes, this was his first solo relic hunt. Yes, it had succeeded more spectacularly than he'd ever imagined—well, check that: he'd imagined plenty of success. It had succeeded as he'd hoped. But that success paled in comparison to the truth of it all. Finding the treasures put his dad at risk. The man who had made Harry what he was. The guy Harry wanted to be. No treasure was worth that.

His boots pounded on the narrow stone walkway. "Slow down," Lauren called out from behind. Harry sped up. He didn't look down, didn't look up, just marched across the twenty-foot chasm without stopping until he reached the far side. Lauren finally caught up. "Are you crazy?" she asked. "Why race across?"

"The sooner I get this stuff for your boss, the sooner I get my dad out of harm's way. You have a problem with that?" Lauren said nothing. "Good. Now don't move while I figure out how to do this without dying."

The three stone pillars stood across from them now. Equally spaced, about waist-high, they were remarkable only for their simplicity. "They're plain stone cylinders," Harry said. "No decoration, no markings, no—hang on. What's that?"

The central pillar had obscured it until now. A small statue, tucked against the back wall, about the height of Harry's knees. A statue of a cloaked woman. "Are those bird wings on her back?" Harry asked.

"Raven's wings," Lauren said, craning her neck to see.

Seems like Lauren knew this figure. "Who is it?"

"You should know," Lauren said. "She saved your life in the caves."

Raven's wings. Of course. "The Morrigan," Harry said. "Why is she here?"

"Look at her hands."

The winged statue's hands were cupped in front of her waist, palms up. "Is she holding something?" Harry asked.

"Not yet. The Morrigan helps warriors gain victory over their enemies. She does this on one condition: that the warrior have humility in his heart. A warrior must serve others, not himself. Only then will she help him."

"Then I hope you're humble. I'm not tops in that department."

"Warriors must be humble, and they must honor her, specifically with a gift. They often left gifts of bread or wine at her altar. However, some warriors left precious objects for her."

The answer came to him. "Looks like you could put a baseball in her hands." He reached into his pocket. "Or a baseball-sized chunk of gold."

"My thoughts exactly." She held her hand out. "I'll do it."

"Be my guest." He gave her the gold. "Don't touch those treasures until you do. Humility, remember?"

Lauren carried the heavy rock in both hands as she walked between the central sword and the cauldron before stooping in front of the small deity. Harry didn't see her put the stone in the goddess's hands. He only saw her jump back.

"It moved!" Lauren shouted and stepped back. "Her hands went down."

Harry shouted back. "Watch the treasures."

Lauren froze, then slowly moved between the pedestals and back to where Harry waited. "Why are you worried about touching them?" she asked. "I put the gold in the correct place."

"What happened?"

"Her hands lowered when I put the gold in them," Lauren said. "They moved straight down. The gold is heavy enough to move them."

"Then don't take it out of her hands, no matter what." Harry pointed at the cauldron. "We get that one first."

"Why?"

"It's the biggest one. You help me carry that across, then we'll each carry one of the others. Make sense?"

Lauren said it did. They went over and examined the pillar with the cauldron, failed to find any indication of traps or hidden levers or other dangerous additions, and then each took a side and lifted. The iron tub was as big as a laundry basket and a hundred times as heavy. Harry could have lifted it himself, but having Lauren's help made it easy going. Walking backwards over the tiny path, however, made him hold his breath. They made it, he exhaled, and they left the cauldron on the ground and went back to the treasures.

"Are you surprised they didn't have any other safeguards in place for these treasures?" Lauren asked.

Harry chose not to mention that this was his very first adventure. "I suspect they figured the spears and death-walk and golden nugget were enough."

Lauren shrugged and walked to the sword. Harry stayed put. Her words had set off a tiny bell inside his head. So soft he could barely hear it, so unexpected he hardly dared acknowledge it, but that bell rang in his head and a voice he had only just discovered whispered a warning. That this wasn't over yet.

"Hang on."

Lauren stopped beside the sword and turned her head. "What is it?"

He tried and failed to come up with an explanation of why the hairs on his neck were on end. "I don't know," he said. "I'm worried."

"We made it, Harry. We did it."

He shook his head. She was right. They'd done it. They were here, the treasures were real, and now he could get out of this mess without his dad getting shot. *Stop worrying and stay the course.* "You're right." He moved to the spear. "Grab these and let's get out of here."

He went and stood in front of the spear. It looked an awful lot like the ones sticking out of Maurice. What was so special about this one? A wooden shaft, an iron point, what used to be leather wrapped around it for grip. Maybe the sword would prove more appealing to the eye, he thought, turning to look at it.

"The blade of Nuada's sword is said to glow," Lauren said. "I hope it's true."

She put her hand on the grip, and his heart dropped as a memory blared for attention. *Only draw the sword to unleash the Morrigan's wrath.* Morrigan, the war deity. And *death*.

Before he could shout a warning, Lauren picked up the sword, still in its scabbard, and held it aloft. As she did so, she turned to see Harry's mouth open in a shout, which was cut off abruptly as an unmistakable noise sounded. The noise of a golden rock falling out of a small goddess's hands.

Lauren's eyes went wide. "What was that?"

The tunnel shook. His vision blurred as forces came alive behind the stone walls. Dust clouds erupted and the golden ball rolled across the floor to bounce off Harry's ankle. A thunderous *crack* split the air and Harry turned to watch a section of the impossibly narrow walkway break off and fall into the pit, leaving a gap in the path. Their only path out of here.

"Run!"

Harry grabbed Lauren's free arm and hauled her after him, the invaluable golden baseball bouncing in front of him as he raced for the disintegrating path. Instinct made him let go of her long enough to scoop up the gold rock and shove it back in his pocket without breaking stride. Still running, he reached back for her outstretched hand and caught it, nearly ripping her arm out of its socket as he accelerated toward a path that was no longer there.

"We have to jump," he shouted before letting go. He never slowed as the deadly chasm came at him, planting his foot on the lip of uncertain stone and launching himself at the other side of the narrow path, which was falling apart as he watched. He hung in the air over nothing but darkness for an eternity, the world quaking and dust coating his throat, before one foot hit the other side and he kept running. Behind him, he could hear Lauren's shouts; they were so loud he knew she must have made it across. Without looking back, he kept going. The weight of the spear was throwing him off balance, and he could hear the stones cracking apart beneath him. Halfway across. *We're going to make it.*

The end of the path broke loose. "Have to jump again!" That was all the warning he could give her before he leapt across the void. Arms spinning, chest heaving, he flew.

He made it. Harry landed on the far side, stumbled and then righted himself.

Lauren smashed into his back and they went down in a heap. He rolled and his head hit something hard. The cauldron. He felt her arms around him as his head rang and his vision blurred. "Get up," Lauren shouted. "Get up."

Something hissed in his ear and dirt flew across his face. Lauren grabbed him by the shoulders and hauled him to his feet before he realized what it was. A spear, fired from the wall. The spears he thought he'd deactivated.

He didn't think. He reacted. "With me!" Harry pulled Lauren close, and with a strength he shouldn't have possessed, lifted the cauldron with one hand and flipped it upside down to trap them both inside, still clutching their prizes.

Lauren didn't need to be told to run. They bolted forward, the cauldron over their heads. They were nearly deafened by a series of metallic bangs, as a hail of spears smashed off the protective shell. It was as though lightning bolts hurled by the gods on high were pummeling them. *Bang. Bang.* Again and again, the explosions scrambled his mind as he forged ahead. He couldn't see, couldn't hear, couldn't do anything but run. Pain burned across his calf in a fiery slash as a spear grazed him. Lauren shouted. Harry ran.

They tripped.

One instant they were hurtling forward. The next the world twisted upside down. Harry's head banged off the inside the cauldron, and then he tumbled backside-over-elbows in a non-stop spinning world of pain. Light pierced his eyes and he squinted them shut, thudding against the ground before sliding to a stop. Dirt filled his nose and dust caked his eyes and his lungs burned hot. He stopped moving, face down, hardly able to breathe.

"Harry!" his dad called out. There was a sound of running feet, and then hands grabbed him and flipped him over, and the air was crushed from his lungs. It took Harry some time to realize his father had him in both arms and was holding him tight. "You made it," Fred said. "I thought I lost you."

Harry gently pushed his dad away and sat up. They were outside the tunnel entrance, sitting in the sun, with the water falling nearby. He coughed. "Nothing to it." He looked down to find the spear still clenched in one hand. "Brought something for you." He offered it to Fred.

Fred grabbed for it so fast he nearly knocked Harry over. "It's their treasure," Fred said. "The treasure of the Tuatha."

Harry managed to get back up and find his feet, and Fred rose, dusting off his trousers.

"Part of it," Harry said. "She has the sword."

His vision cleared and he discovered that Tom stood beside Lauren, looking at but not touching the sword. Just beyond them, Maurice's body lay where it had fallen. *That's what we tripped on.* He kept the thought to himself.

Sunlight flashed off a gun barrel. "Hand the spear to me."

Tom had his pistol aimed at Fred. "Do it now."

Fred frowned. "Take it. My son and I don't want your treasure."

Tom leaned over and snatched it. "Then you should have stayed out of Ireland."

"We're leaving." Fred looked at Harry. "Come on, son. They can have it all."

"Not so fast." Tom waggled his gun at Fred. "I can't have you tell anyone what we found. Not yet."

"I'm not saying anything," Fred said. "Neither is my son."

"I know you won't," Tom said. "The same as Maurice won't. You are the reason he's dead. I can't let that go."

Sunlight flashed off metal. Tom pulled the trigger and a gunshot boomed.

Dust erupted at Harry's feet and a bullet buried itself in the earth by his toe. Harry looked up. He didn't speak. No one did, except Lauren. "No."

There was a dull clang. Tom's gun lay on the ground and Tom yelped, sucking on suddenly bloodied knuckles. Behind him, Lauren held the sword in a two-handed grip. Expertly, she swung the sword through the rest of its arc, then stepped around in front of him and placed the tip of the blade on his chest. The Irish leader stared at her with his mouth agape. "What are you doing?"

"What is right." She kicked Tom's pistol into the pool of water nearby. "They helped us. They're unarmed. You aren't going to kill them."

Tom stared at her, not moving, his eyes wide open. "I see." He didn't yell, didn't try to fight her. Instead, he collected himself and stood straight. "Now I understand."

Lauren frowned and lowered her sword. "Understand what?"

"How your ancestors conquered this island." Tom stepped back and went to one knee. "Allow me to be the first to say congratulations, Your Highness. The treasures have been restored to the rightful leader of Ireland. Long live the Queen."

Epilogue

*B*rooklyn
Two Days Later

"Welcome home, Harry. Come in, come in."

Rich cigar smoke tickled Harry's nose as he entered Vincent Morello's office. A thick line of the noxious fumes rose from the end of the cigar in the oversized glass ashtray. The head of New York's five families rose from his chair, navigated his way around a desk that may have been a battleship in a prior life, and put his hands on Harry's shoulders. Keen eyes in an elegantly weathered face looked at Harry with pride. "I understand you have been busy," Vincent said.

Harry shrugged. "It was a nice trip, Mr. Morello."

The bushy white hedgerows that Vincent called eyebrows moved. "It's Vincent, please. I am grateful you are safe. Have a seat."

Harry took a seat in one of the chairs across from Vincent's monstrous desk. He held a small bag with both hands, resting it on his lap. A heavy bag. "Thank you for inviting me, Mr. Morello." Vincent had told Harry to call him by his first name many times. Harry never did. Not after his father had explained that with Mr. Morello, it was all about respect.

"Your father did not share many details of your journey," Vincent said. "What did you discover?"

Harry offered the highlights of his activities in Ireland, beginning with a falling bridge in a cave and ending with the discoveries he'd made near, under or across a lake from a series of stone circles. Vincent didn't interrupt, didn't ask questions, didn't do anything but listen. Only when Harry concluded with his narrow escape by the waterfall did Vincent speak.

"You left the ancient Irish artifacts in Ireland?" Vincent asked.

"I believe those relics are with the right people," Harry said.

Lines appeared at the corners of Vincent's eyes. "A wise decision. Those artifacts are part of their heritage. It is only right they keep them. Your graciousness shows respect."

"I didn't leave everything behind." Harry set the bag he carried on Vincent's desk with an audible *thud*. "For you, Mr. Morello."

If Vincent was impressed with the baseball-sized chunk of gold that came out of the bag, he did a good job of hiding it. Fred Fox had probably told him what to expect. Harry made a mental note to chide his father for stealing Harry's thunder. "Thank you," Vincent said. "I will not forget this."

A rock of gold was nothing compared to having Vincent Morello on your side. Harry dipped his chin in acknowledgment as a voice sounded from the hallway outside Vincent's office door. Heavy footsteps followed, and a moment later a mountain filled the doorway. A grinning mountain that couldn't have looked happier.

"Come in," Vincent said to his primary bodyguard, the aptly named Mack. "See what Harry brought back from Ireland."

"Aladdin!" Mack spread arms bigger than Harry's thighs out wide as he walked in. "I heard youse was back in town."

Harry stood and found himself struggling for air when Mack embraced him. He'd learned to ride the hugs out, letting the big man decide when Harry should breathe again. Thankfully, Mack let go in mere seconds. "Good to see you too," Harry said.

"Wouldja look at this." Mack let out a low whistle when he spotted the gold. "Nice rock."

"A generous gift for the family," Vincent said.

Mack nodded his agreement. "Have any close scrapes?" he asked Harry.

"A few."

Mack offered his booming laugh, a comforting sound. "I bet you gave 'em what for." Knuckles cracked as Mack made a fist and shook it. "Nobody messes with a Morello man."

A new voice entered the discussion. "Which Morello do you mean?"

Everyone turned toward the office door. Gelled hair, well-cut clothes, and a presence that carried across rooms. Joey Morello, sole heir of the Morello family, had arrived.

"Harry," Mack said, "had a real adventure and came back with the treasure to prove it."

Mack pointed at the gold. Joey looked at it for a long moment. "A nice recovery," Joey said. "Congratulations."

"Thanks." Harry looked at Joey. Joey looked at Harry, then at his father. "I'd like to speak with you when you're free," Joey said.

Harry took the hint. "I was just about to leave." He stood from his chair. "Thank you for the time, Mr. Morello."

"So soon?" Vincent asked. "You only just returned. Would you care for coffee, or something stronger?"

"Thank you, but I've taken enough of your time." He dipped his head slightly. "I have a few loose ends to wrap up."

Vincent stood, came around the desk and offered his hand. "A fine job, Harry. The first of many, I am sure."

A tingle ran up Harry's back as he shook hands and turned to leave. Impressing Vincent Morello was no mean feat. He glanced at Joey, who looked at him. Silence filled the air for several seconds until Mack offered his congratulations. Harry thanked him. That's when Joey stepped aside to let Harry pass through the door.

"Yes," Joey said. "Nice work. The family thanks you."

Harry murmured his appreciation. Joey did not extend his hand, letting Harry pass by without another word. He walked down the hallway, past the ever-present guard manning the front door, and out into the Brooklyn summer sun. It took him ten minutes at a slow pace to reach his father's house, and he passed a half-dozen people he knew by name on the way. The front door was open when he climbed the stairs, and the screen door banging shut behind him announced Harry's arrival.

Fred called out at the noise. "I'm in the office."

Harry found his dad seated behind a desk. He looked up from his laptop when Harry walked in. "How did the meeting go?" Fred asked.

"Vincent was Vincent." Harry took one of two chairs at a small table. "He doesn't get too excited about much of anything. He did say he wouldn't forget it."

Fred raised an eyebrow. "Is that so? In that case, well done, my boy. Vincent doesn't hand out praise lightly. Did he say anything about the Irish relics?"

"He felt we'd made the right decision to leave them in Ireland. The relics are part of the Irish people's heritage. They belong with them."

"Did you say anything about Lauren?"

The last glimpse Harry had had of the Tuatha's treasures was when Lauren and Tom put them in the back of a massive van that arrived near the Uragh Stone Circle shortly after their harrowing escape from the tunnel. Tom's attitude had changed entirely after he told Lauren the truth about their organization. A truth that had sent her to her backside on the ground in disbelief.

Lauren had looked confused when Tom had knelt before her. "What's wrong with you?" she'd asked.

Tom had then shared the true story of their group. Of how the Irish Heritage Society had existed in one form or another since the day when Romans arrived in Brittania to subdue the unruly inhabitants. Those men and women had resisted, refusing to bend the knee to the mighty Roman Empire, and their resistance had given birth to a secret organization dedicated to ensuring that what had happened to so many other cultures would not happen in Ireland. Tom and Lauren's ancestors swore to fight back and to protect the treasures of the Tuatha Dé Danann, and fight back they did.

However, the fight did not go well. The men who secreted the three treasures were killed shortly after completing their duties, while the tablet detailing where to begin a recovery quest went missing for reasons unknown. That tablet had remained missing for two thousand years until a Pakistani-American guy from Brooklyn found it and realized what he had.

Tom revealed their group had one duty beyond protecting and eventually recovering the treasures. They served as guardians of a secret: the true king. Or queen, in this case. The descendants of the true Irish monarch were watched over by the Irish Historical Society, protected and guarded until the time when they could reclaim their throne. Time and circumstance, however, had turned the world upside down so that now Ireland was hardly recognizable compared to when the Romans invaded, though the claim remained the same.

Centuries ago, Lauren Brosnan's ancestors had ruled the land. If their Society had its way, she would rule once again.

Lauren could only shake her head. Any questions she asked were gently brushed aside; Tom had clearly not wanted to discuss too much in front of the American interlopers. That refusal seemed to set Lauren back on track.

"Fine," she'd said to Tom. "My questions can wait. Helping these two cannot."

Tom gestured toward Harry and Fred. "Helping them do what?"

"Whatever they need. I would be dead if it wasn't for Harry. They didn't cause Maurice's death, and they're not at fault for what happened. Harry followed the tablet clues, the same as we would have." She turned to Harry. "Thank you for everything you've done. I'm sorry I lied to you."

"No worries," Harry said. "I'm sorry about Maurice."

"We will remember him." Lauren appeared to stand a little straighter, and her voice seemed to come out a little stronger. Perhaps she had been that way all along and he'd never noticed. "You'll always have a friend on our island." She offered a hand. "I swear it."

"Thanks," Harry said as they shook. "What will you do now?"

Lauren looked across a lush, rolling landscape of the most brilliant green to be found anywhere in the world. A green unique to Ireland. "Fulfill my destiny."

She'd left him with that. Harry and Fred were free to go, taking the golden rock as thanks, and though he had little idea how Lauren intended to fulfill whatever she felt her destiny might be, he wouldn't bet against her.

They parted ways not long afterwards. Men working for Tom carried Maurice's corpse away and loaded it into the back of their vehicle, along with the cauldron and spear. The sword remained in its scabbard, clasped tightly in Lauren's hands. Tom didn't reveal the truth about Lauren to the men, at least not that Harry saw, and in short order Harry and his father were on the first plane back to New York. That had been two days ago.

"I didn't say anything about her," Harry said to his dad. "Didn't think it mattered to Vincent."

"Building connections can be more valuable than any amount of gold," Fred said. "I'll let Vincent know the Irish Historical Society owes a debt to you. He will appreciate that."

Harry added an entry to his mental notebook. Connections. Make them. Keep them. Perhaps, in the future, even use them. "Mack was excited about the gold," Harry said. "As you'd expect."

Fred waited a few beats. "Did you see Joey?"

Another few beats. "I did," Harry said.

"What did he say?"

"Not much."

Fred tapped a finger on his desk. "Don't worry about it. He's a good person with a lot on his shoulders."

Harry cleared his throat. "What happens now? I gave Vincent the gold. We don't have anything to call Rose Leroux about. What's next?"

Harry's experience with his father's world had been consistent in many ways. Fred Fox recovered or located an artifact, occasionally finding it in the field, more often working with collectors to buy, sell or trade for it. The business side went through New York's premier fence of black-market goods, a lady named Rose Leroux whom even Vincent Morello never crossed. Rose was an enigma, a woman who knew everyone and everything about them, and if Harry had to describe her, the only thing he could say with certainty was that history was littered with the bones of men who had crossed Rose Leroux.

"That depends." Fred pointed the tapping finger at Harry. "What do you want to do?"

"Me?" Harry frowned. "I don't know."

"You are many things," Fred said. "Indecisive is not one of them. What do you want to do next?" Harry couldn't think of a single thing and he said so. "Here's a suggestion," Fred said. "Listen to your father for a few minutes." Harry said that was fine. "What I do after any time in the field is consider what I learned," Fred said. "Everything is a learning experience. Intelligent people build on their experiences, remember their mistakes, and learn from them. Tell me what you learned."

If it worked for his father, it would work for Harry. How else would he ever expect to hold his own in the field? "Be careful who you trust," Harry said. "That's the main one."

"Good start. Don't confuse being cautious with never trusting anyone. You can't do it alone all the time."

"How do you know when to trust someone?"

"Excellent lead-in to what should be lesson number two." Fred pointed at Harry's navel. "Trust your gut."

"It told me to follow the first tablet into a cave. That nearly got me killed."

"'Nearly' being the operative word. That instinct inside you is like a muscle. It gets better the more you use it." Fred put his hands up. "If you want my advice, find another career. Don't be like me. It's dangerous." Fred's voice lowered. "I didn't grow up wanting to be a relic hunter."

I did. Harry didn't say it out loud. He didn't need to. His dad knew what Harry wanted. And why. "I'm still working on what my career will be," Harry said. "This is a quiet interlude to tide me over until I decide."

"As you wish. A bold decision, but not necessarily unintelligent. Which is important. Be bold. Take risks. But don't take them unnecessarily." He must have noted the confusion on Harry's face. "Another way to say it would be 'Make sure the juice is worth the squeeze.'"

"Makes sense when you put it like that," Harry said. He waited. Fred watched him wait. "Is that it?" Harry asked. "Any other lessons?"

"Two or three are plenty for one adventure. These sorts of lessons are best learned in the field. If you want them to stick, get out and chase a few relics. Speaking of which, I hope you are ready for some time off before you go gallivanting around again."

Harry grinned. "Gallivanting sounds like more fun."

"I was afraid you'd say that." Fred opened a manila folder on his desk and removed a single sheet of paper. "As luck would have it, something came up. I'm working on an acquisition for Vincent. A Roman-era bust, and I'll be traveling to Italy several times in the coming month, which leaves me no time to look into this."

Fred pushed the paper over toward Harry, who got up and went to get it. He found a colorful image on the top half of the sheet, an image of a familiar individual. "Lots of precious stones," Harry said. "But the statue may not appeal to everyone."

A small caption gave the details. The statue was made of solid gold, covered with emeralds, rubies and sapphires, and depicted a mythical figure known across the world. Harry held the paper closer to his face. "Are the snakes made of jade?"

"The highest-quality jade you can imagine," Fred said. "The most beautiful statue of Medusa ever crafted."

A Gorgon from Greek mythology. One of three monstrous sisters capable of turning anyone who looked at them to stone, Medusa was a woman with snakes for hair, alternately depicted as hideous or beautiful, and usually described as harboring a burning hatred of mortal men. "Plenty of gemstones on the piece," Harry said. "Is this Greek?"

"Second-century BCE," Fred said. "Considered by many to be the finest example of Greek craftsmanship of the era. Which makes it even more disappointing that no one knows where it is."

Harry looked up from the photo of the incredible statue. "No one?"

Fred winked. "No one except me, and I'm too busy to go find it. Know anyone who might be interested?"

Harry went back to his chair and sat down. "Where do I begin?"

Author's Note

This adventure revolves around the Midsummer celebration, and I'll admit that before I started writing this I knew very little (read, nothing) about this ancient tradition other than a vague idea it may tie to megalithic structures such as Stonehenge. Not entirely wrong, but close enough that I wouldn't get any points for my efforts.

The true origins of Midsummer stretch back to the Neolithic era, which began roughly twelve thousand years ago. The main purpose of the Midsummer celebration – at least in regards to this story – is to mark the summer solstice, which is the day of the year in the Northern Hemisphere with the longest day and shortest night. Typically this is around June 20th or June 21st in my part of the world. Today the celebration is mostly what I'd call niche, a neat fact to tell my kids before I force them to go to sleep with the sun still up. However, for certain people and belief systems, it is much, much more. People in this book whom I refer to as pagans quite often, a term I have no intent to use in a pejorative fashion, to be clear. That being said, let's get into what I'm starting to learn is the best part of the book for many readers – which is great!

Harry's first solo expedition in the field finds him traipsing through and somewhat wrecking Dunmore Cave (*Chapter 1*). This designated National Monument is open to the public and can be found referenced in Irish written records going back over five hundred years, when it was noted as being one of the "three darkest places in Ireland". Not the sort of place you'd want to venture into without a friend is how I take that. And certainly not when you consider what happened there in 928 ADE.

One thousand men, women and children were massacred by Viking invaders. Human remains uncovered in the cave are potentially those of massacre victims, with one theory as to their fate being that these victims asphyxiated when the Vikings set fires to smoke them out of the caves. In addition, the hoard of silver and bronze coins is real, having been located in 1999. Readers who enjoy the *Indiana Jones* movies may also recognize the ships I describe inside the caves which aid in Harry uncovering the tablet; these are Roman triremes, and I included this specific type of ship as an ode to this type of ship being a crucial part of the ending to *Indiana Jones and the Dial of Destiny*. In truth, it's highly unlikely that such ships would have served to inspire anything in Ireland other than fear.

The Tuatha Dé Danann legend (*Chapter 1*) is a mesmerizing story from Irish myth. The story as detailed in Harry's quest is true, as are the four treasures. The Stone of Fal is on the Hill of Tara and is as described, though the nearby castle Harry ventures into was created for story purposes—I needed him to get high enough to see over that hill. The other three treasures (Lugh's Spear, Nuada's Sword and Dagda's Cauldron) are, to the best of my knowledge, still missing. Which is not the same as mythical.

A crucial piece of Harry's initial research into the treasures required understanding the goddess Danu, specifically that she is a sun goddess, which allows him to decipher how to proceed. While Danu is part of the Irish myth—the translation of Tuatha Dé Danann is typically listed as "the folk of the goddess Danu"—shockingly little is known about her beyond this reference. She is not mentioned anywhere else at all in the myths, so we have no idea if she was a sun goddess. For our story, though, I gave her that honor.

This is also where Harry begins to learn about Midsummer. While it was a significant holiday in Ireland (or what would become Ireland) at the time, it was not the only holiday. However, vital to this story, it was truly co-opted (that may be a bit of a strong term, but not too far from the truth) by the Romans and then the Christians as I detail in the story. What we do today, the books we read, the stories we tell, the music we blast in our cars, none of it is new. It's all based on a line or lyric someone heard a long time ago, absorbed, and then used as inspiration to create their own art. We are built on our past, and that's as true for holidays as it is for anything else.

For story purposes, I also made the Fal Stone quite a bit larger than it truly is, and I added the markings on it as well, and though there is a church on the Hill of Tara, it is not like the one I describe. One other deviation from pseudo-fact is that the sword does not necessarily represent or only unleash death, it is supposedly irresistible, drawing every man and woman to it. The Celtic Cross at the Hill of Tara is real, but it's nowhere near as large as I make it out to be, and the only thing any shadows or sunlight falling through the openings will touch is grass. The castle is also a creation for story purposes, as is the subterranean chamber containing a stone tablet. Unless it's so well-hidden no one has found it, of course. If you happen to be in the area and stumble across any previously unknown locations, proceed with care, dear reader.

The town of Kealkill (*Chapter 9*) is a rustic, small affair, with two notable historical events to its name. One is that the first fatalities of the Irish Civil War happened in Kealkill. The other is that a long time ago a stone circle was erected near the town. Five stones planted upright in the dirt, with two others nearby, the purposes of which are a mystery. While a fantastic archaeological site, the circle is one of many across Ireland and doesn't stand out in most ways. I changed that for our story by adding the spear stone that led Harry to this Kealkill Circle, along with a Celtic cross as well as an ancient well. If there is a well in the vicinity, it has not yet been found, so any booby-trapped tunnels complete with flaming stone balls or other hazards would still be waiting for an unwary adventurer. As to the origins of Midsummer which are discussed by Harry and Lauren at the site, the truth is we simply can't say with any certainty where Brittonic Midsummer truly originated, for the simple fact very few written records survive from the ancient Britons, which makes the past a very murky place.

Inside the tunnel in Kealkill Harry finds two images carved in a wall while a flaming ball bears down on him after he's trapped inside a giant cage. Fortunately, two images on a wall test his knowledge of the Irish myth of Aed, killed by a man named Corrgend, and Harry passes the test. According to some versions of the legend Corrgend was tasked by the gods with finding an appropriate tombstone for Aed. Lucky for Corrgend he found one. Unlucky for Corrgend? His heart exploded when he lifted the massive rock. My money is on the gods knew this might happen.

The next clue tied to an Irish myth Harry encounters involves Nuada and an arm lost in battle (*Chapter 11*). Harry discovers an engraving on a stone circle in Kealkill that points the way forward, an engraving of Nuada's arm. There are no carvings related to Nuada on any stone circle in Kealkill, though the myth as outlined in their deductions is accurate. Nuada was the first king of the Tuatha Dé Danann, at least until his arm was chopped off in battle. These mythical beings weren't keen on their leaders being less than perfect, which sadly for Nuada applied even if you lost your arm (and therefore, your perfection) in battle defending your people. As luck would have it, Nuada obtained a replacement arm—solid silver, supposedly—from another mythical god. Perfection restored, he regained his throne. This section of the quest again involves the goddess Danu, about whom very little is known despite her being part of the name for these mythical beings. The association between Danu and both motherhood and agriculture is real, though I focus more heavily than may be warranted on the good weather and productive harvest portions of her for story purposes.

One of the quirkier facts I uncovered while researching this story involves the Feast of Saint John and how Romans calculated the day for celebrating this event (*Chapter 11*). Rome didn't become the foremost power of the day by subjugation alone. Cajoling, assimilation and occasionally even acceptance aided their quest for domination. Acceptance in the form of allowing conquered people to continue worshipping their gods. However, that wasn't always the case. What's better than freely allowing defeated people to worship their own gods? Convince them your gods aren't any different than theirs and allow them to assimilate on their own.

Some argue this is exactly what Christianity did when it created this holiday around the fourth or fifth century, taking...inspiration (*cough, cough)* from pagan Midsummer celebrations. The day of June 24 is an odd choice. Why is it odd? Because Romans counted days by counting *backwards* from the preceding month. This matters because Romans had Christmas set as the eighth day before January 1, which is December 24. Go back to the middle of the year (July 2), count back eight days, and you land on June 24—one day before the middle day of the year. Harry's summary of how Christianity co-opted a pagan holiday as its own is almost certainly accurate.

Readers who have enjoyed Harry's future adventures will be familiar with at least one other waterfall tied to a lost relic, an Austrian location that features in a James Bond movie which grabbed my eye and demanded to be included in Harry's world. That may be the root of why I created the waterfall (*Chapter 14*) near the Uragh Stone Circle; it doesn't exist in real life, but I think it's a fun detail that adds to the story. The body of water adjacent to the Stone Circle is real, as is the Circle, though there are no carvings present of Nuada pointing to hidden treasure.

Harry and Lauren ultimately recover the trio of lost treasures of the Tuatha Dé Danann (*Chapter 16*). Treasures which proved to be far less interesting than the woman who found them. A direct descendant of the original Irish Kings? Far-fetched, perhaps, but not impossible. The true story of the High Kings of Ireland is borderline impenetrable once you go back to the times when Roman forces invaded Brittania, with the factual (and I use the term in a historical sense here, which is to say no one's truly certain) and verifiable Kings of Ireland only being on record beginning around the mid-fifth century, which is three to four hundred years after the Roman's initial attempts at a conquest of Ireland. At that time Ireland was quite divided, with local chieftains calling themselves Kings, though their kingdoms would have been rather small. However, these bands and tribes managed to stand up to the Roman forces—with no small measure of help from horribly inhospitable terrain and erratic weather—and Rome never truly conquered Ireland. What the Empire did succeed in accomplishing was furthering the spread of Christianity by stamping out the pagan religions, so much so that in the mid-fifth century one of Christianity's most recognizable figures spread his beliefs across Ireland with such success that he is now inextricably linked with the land and known as the "Apostle of Ireland". That would be Saint Patrick, of course, a man who has sold more beer than anyone in history.

But Patrick was no High King. The first generally recognized High King of Ireland doesn't arrive until 459 CE, with everyone before him a mix of legend, lost manuscripts, and half-truths. In other words, these men probably existed, led a tribe or clan, but weren't true kings as we understand them today, men who led entire nations. These legendary High Kings trace their authority back to the very beginnings of Ireland, to the Tuatha Dé Danann, whose reign supposedly began around 1477 BCE, or two thousand years before any reliable information exists.

We do know someone led tribes in Ireland. Probably quite a few people, in fact, and when Constantine and Sylvester were around and scheming to expand their power, as powerful men are wont to do, there probably would have been an Irish leader powerful enough to serve as a representative for his island. Who's to say he didn't have the lost treasures of the Tuatha to serve as his earthly proof of divine right to lead? If he did, maybe he realized the Romans were coming for him and his beliefs, so perhaps he decided to secret those objects away for safekeeping, hidden until the time was right for them to return. It's possible he left a trail for true believers to follow. A trail that has not yet been found.

And the most important "what if" of all?

What if his living descendant is a she? A she ready to assume the dormant crown and give Ireland a new Queen?

I think that would be neat. And it would make a heck of a story.

Thanks for joining me on this adventure as Harry learned about the origins of Midsummer and took his first steps toward becoming the world's foremost relic hunter. More treasures and explorations into the origins of our favorite holidays await, and I can't wait to share them with you.

I couldn't do this without you, the reader. You are truly the best.

Andrew Clawson
November 2025

Excerpt from The All Hallows' Icon

You can get your copy of THE ALL HALLOWS' ICON on Amazon.

Chapter 1

Florence, Italy

A giant nearly crushed Harry Fox underfoot.

"Watch it!" Harry barked as he jumped back to avoid a muscle-bound arm and offered a few choice words. The man stopped. He turned to face Harry. Who began to regret his choice of words.

The big brute leaned toward Harry just as a long selfie stick pushed between them and a pair of Asian women chattering excitedly swept through without a glance at either man. Harry Fox knew the sound of opportunity knocking. He took his chance and darted behind a group of tourists gathered around a guide speaking French. Harry only turned once those dozen tourists stood between him and the big guy, looking back to find the man offering Harry one final glower before he went on his way.

"This piazza's huge and you manage to run into me," Harry muttered to himself. Softly, taking no chance the big guy might hear him. "Lucky I have business to handle."

Even Harry didn't believe his bluster. He headed across the Piazza della Signora, the open square fronting the fourteenth-century town hall of Florence. The scent of rich espresso ran across his nose while conversations in multiple languages could be heard around him. Harry narrowed his gaze on one statue ahead. A statue of a stark-naked man with a head of curly hair and a body known across the globe. It was a copy of the original sculpture nearby.

"Afternoon, David." Harry spoke to the statue as he approached. "You see my guy?"

The statue did not reply. Harry slowed as he approached the giant replica, looking at and then past every single person around David. Not at their faces. He looked at their heads. Or rather, what sat atop their heads. A flash of yellow caught his attention. "Found you."

Harry Fox had come to Florence to make a purchase. The seller promised to wear a bright yellow hat so Harry wouldn't miss him in the crowd. A crowd Harry insisted on being in when this deal went down. Not because he didn't trust this seller. Because his dad told him not to trust anyone.

A couple took pictures in front of the replica of David as Harry circled around to stand in front of the man in the yellow hat now at David's rear. The tall pedestal holding the statue cast yellow hat in shadow. A metal case that could have held a guitar rested against the pedestal. Yellow hat kept two hands on the case. A case he had good reason to keep close, for what it contained would soon bring him a lot of money.

Harry looked to either side before posing a question. "Did you come alone?"

Oskar Bulka, he of the yellow hat, nodded. "I did."

Harry nodded to the case. "Open it," Harry said.

Oskar flicked several latches and then indicated for Harry to come closer. "I do not think you want all these people to see it too," Oskar said. "I wish we did not meet here."

What Oskar wanted was not Harry's concern. "Keep it out of sight," Harry said.

Oskar did as asked, their bodies shielding the case from view as Harry opened it far enough so he could see inside. He drew in a breath, then let it out in a slow whistle. "It's gorgeous."

Three feet of steel gleamed. Nestled inside the velvet-lined cased, the sword looked sharp enough to inflict serious damage. Not bad for a piece of metal crafted nearly two thousand years ago. Harry opened the lid further and angled his head to get a better look at the inscriptions on the blade's center. His lips moved silently as he translated the Latin. "Exactly as you described it," Harry said before he closed the case and reached into his coat pocket, coming out with a thick envelope. "Fifty thousand euros, as agreed."

Oskar put the envelope inside his jacket, furtively checking the stack of five-hundred-euro notes for several moments before tucking them away. Not that Harry watched him. He was too busy staring at the sword.

A Roman spatha, the straight sword favored by heavy infantry in the Roman Empire. This sword had clearly never seen combat. Harry could have picked up a similar sword for a fraction of the price without leaving Brooklyn, yet he'd traveled across an ocean to meet a Polish dealer while carrying a small fortune in cash to buy this specific sword. Why? Because this weapon had been a gift from an Emperor. Constantine the Great had ordered this sword crafted as a gift to the Pagan tribal leader of what would eventually become Great Britain, though at the time it was a wild and untamed land populated by various tribes who constantly warred with each other. Yes, Julius Caesar had invaded Britain some two hundred years before, and future Roman leaders continued the quest to subjugate the Britons with varying degrees of success, but when faced with Constantine's legions the native Britons decided to give peace a try. They came to him seeking peace, offering gifts along with their promises, so Constantine offered his own gift in return.

This spatha. A sword unlike any other, Constantine told the Pagan King that this gift was the Sword of Fionn mac Cumhaill. A clever move, naming the sword after a legendary myth in which Fionn slayed a fire-breathing assailant one day each year – a day held dear by the Britons. The sword was decorated with symbols of the pagan holiday Samhain. Although this sword represented the promise of peace, history, however, would prove this promise false. This spatha marked the beginning of the end of the Britons way of life. It was a deception they did not see coming.

Oskar's voice pulled Harry from his thoughts. "We have a deal?"

Harry closed the case. "We do." He stuck one hand out. "Pleasure doing—"

"Give me the case."

A shadow fell over Harry as a man stepped close to him. Harry looked up. All the way up until he found the face of a man he hoped to never see again. The giant who'd nearly run him over. Fire burned in Harry's gut. "Piss off."

The man stood a foot taller than Harry. He did not piss off, but reached under his shirt and put one meaty hand on the handle of a very big pistol. "I said give me the case."

A small part of Harry's brain not shouting at him to run noted the man's Italian accent even as the guy spoke English. He knew Harry and Oskar understood him. Somehow, he knew. "You want it?" Harry asked. "Fine." He made a show of reaching slowly into the case. "You don't need the gun. I'm not getting shot over this thing."

The big man's hand came ever-so-slightly off the pistol. Harry glanced at Oskar. Every bit of color had drained from his face. Oskar knows this guy. Harry played a hunch. "You're the guy I outbid." He had no idea if there had been a bidding war.

"Wrong." The big man shook his head. "He refused to sell."

Oskar found a shadow of his voice. "I do not sell to fascists." His eyes narrowed and he spat at the ground. "Werewolf scum."

The big man growled but kept his eyes on Harry. "Hand it over."

Fascists? Werewolf? Harry filed that away. That could matter if he survived this. "Easy," Harry said, his hand now inside the case. "You can have it." His fingers wrapped around the sword's handle and he lifted it free. "Just don't—"

He whipped the blade out and sliced at the big man's hand. Steel flashed, the big man moved, and Harry's arm shuddered as though he'd sliced into a brick wall. Too late he realized the flat of the blade had smashed into the big man's arm instead of a sharp edge. Big man shouted, the gun went flying, and before Harry could react the big guy's other arm came out of nowhere. An open palm smashed into the side of Harry's skull and sent him stumbling toward Oskar. Harry slammed into the Polish seller as a grisly noise sounded.

The sword was buried halfway into Oskar's stomach. Osker's eyes bulged and his mouth hung open as he slumped against the pedestal. Movement in the corner of Harry's eye made him duck. The big man's fist whizzed through the air above his head as Harry pulled the sword free from Oskar's corpse. He turned to find not a single person even looking at the unfolding disaster, so he ran.

Directly into a group of tourists not ten feet away. German curses filled the air as people flew in all directions. Harry rolled as he hit the ground, popped up to his feet and kept moving. A glance back found the big man rumbling through, hot on Harry's tail.

Thick white columns flashed by on one side as he raced through a narrow street. Metal scaffolding groaned on the other side, Harry sprinting past groups of pedestrians as the sound of his footsteps echoed off the tall buildings to either side while the big man kept close. A woman pointed at Harry, her mouth open. The sword. His hand still clasped the weapon, bloody for anyone to see. He jammed it inside his jacket without breaking stride. Hand-drawn caricatures propped on pedestals nearly went flying as he veered around yet another barricade cordoning off a construction zone. Beeping sounded as Harry looked back. Beeping he ignored.

Until he ran headfirst into the side of a reversing van. The door seemed to throw him back, his world spinning as the ground raced up and crashed into his backside. He bounced up as pain coursed through his entire body, everything aching as he regained his feet, ignored the now honking horn and bolted around the front of the van toward an archway beyond. Two security guards stood at the head of a queue of people lined up behind the columns. They never even looked over at the pursuit.

The Uffizi. A line of people waited to enter Florence's world-renowned gallery, where the real David could be seen. Harry raced beneath an archway. The Arno River blocked his path ahead. He hung a hard right, his boots skidding on the stone street as he took the turn without slowing. Loud cursing and shouting followed moments later when the big man ignored the laws of physics and tried to make the same turn without success.

An elderly couple eating gelato stared wide-eyed as Harry raced past. A colorful graffiti tag on a rolling metal door flashed by on one side, the river sparkling ahead as the sun came out on the other. Harry swerved around a slow-moving cyclist and saw what waited. Closed-in shops running across a bridge known across the globe. The Ponte Vecchio.

The only Florentine bridge not destroyed in World War II, it had jewelers, art dealers and souvenir sellers running its length on either side. What caught Harry's eye as he turned onto the bridge was a way to save his neck.

A metal fire escape along the shop on one end led to a window on the top floor. Harry leapt up and grabbed the lowest rung, which was retracted well above ground level. The big guy shouldn't be able to jump that high. Get to the top, lose the brute and be — bang.

The metal ladder rung slid down to ground level. Harry moved up the ladder to the first landing and turned to pull the ladder up after him, out of reach.

Too late. The big man had hold of the lower rung and was on his way up.

Harry pounded up to the second landing, his legs shouting in protest as the metal rattled and the big guy kept pace. Harry made it to the next ladder which led to the top landing. A closed window waited there. Harry's gaze went to the gutter above him. It looked sturdy. This better work.

Harry jumped, grabbed hold of the gutter and pulled. The gutter held. He pulled himself up, swinging his torso over the edge and kicking to get one leg on the roof. One leg made it. The other did not.

"Got you!"

The big guy grabbed hold of Harry's dangling leg. Harry kicked, the man held on, then pulled. Harry's muscles burned as he clutched to keep hold of the terra cotta roof tiles. Forget this. His jaw went tight as Harry let his other leg dangle back over the roof edge, pulled his foot up, and smashed it down about where the big man's head should be. Nothing but air. He slid a bit lower, pulled his leg back and gave it a second go. Direct hit. The big guy howled as he let go of Harry's leg, and Harry whipped himself up onto the rooftop.

A view of Florence stretched out around him. The Arno waters dazzled in the sunlight, a single boat puttering down the river and pedestrians on the sidewalk. Harry turned and ran.

And immediately slipped. A roof tile shot out from under his foot and he crashed down, getting up a beat later and trying to run. He made it one step before the big man grabbed hold of his collar. Harry reached into his jacket, grabbed the sword and spun, using the flat side of the blade like a club.

The thud of metal hitting bone reached Harry's ears a moment before the big man fell sideways over the roof edge. Harry leapt as the sword clattered across the tiles and followed the big man over the edge.

"No!"

Harry shouted as the sword slipped from his grasp and chased the falling man into the river, slicing through the water to vanish from sight.

The first pedestrians shouted, pointing at a man splashing around in the water. Harry kept low as he spun around and crawled toward the bridge side of the roof to where a drain pipe waited. He flipped over the gutter edge, grabbed hold of the drain pipe and descended hand-over-hand until he could drop to onto the Ponte Vecchio bridge.

He landed directly beside a woman wearing enough diamonds to ransom a duke. Harry dipped his chin. "Afternoon."

The woman gaped as Harry turned and calmly walked into the crowd. First, get away from here. Next, do what he really didn't want to. Call his dad. Harry shook his head as he moved. Dad's not going to like this.

To continue the story, you can purchase a copy of THE ALL HALLOWS' ICON on Amazon.

***

GET YOUR COPY OF THE HARRY FOX STORY THE NAPOLEON CIPHER, AVAILABLE EXCLUSIVELY FOR MY VIP READER LIST

Sharing the writing journey with my readers is a special privilege. I love connecting with anyone who reads my stories, and one way I accomplish that is through my mailing list. I only send notices of new releases or the occasional special offer related to my novels.

If you sign up for my VIP reader mailing list, I'll send you a copy of The Napoleon Cipher, the Harry Fox adventure that's not sold in any store. You can get your copy of this exclusive novel by signing up at my website.

***

Did you enjoy this story? Let people know

Reviews are the most effective way to get my books noticed. I'm one guy, a small fish in a massive pond. Over time, I hope to change that, and I would love your help. The best thing you could do to help spread the word is leave a review on your platform of choice.

Honest reviews are like gold. If you've enjoyed this book I would be so grateful if you could take a few minutes leaving a review, short or long.

Thank you very much.

Also by

Also by Andrew Clawson

***

Harry Fox Origin Stories
The Midsummer Treasures
The All Hallows' Icon

***

Harry Fox Adventures
The Arthurian Relic
The Emerald Tablet
The Celtic Quest
The Achilles Legend
The Pagan Hammer
The Pharaoh's Amulet
The Thracian Idol
The Antikythera Code
The Charlemagne Accord

The Centurion's Spear

***

The Parker Chase Series
A Patriot's Betrayal
The Crowns Vengeance
Dark Tides Rising
A Republic of Shadows
A Hollow Throne
A Tsar's Gold

***

The TURN Series
TURN: The Conflict Lands
TURN: A New Dawn
TURN: Endangered

About the author

Andrew Clawson is the author of multiple series, including the Parker Chase and TURN thrillers, as well as the Harry Fox adventures.

You can find him at his website, AndrewClawson.com, or you can connect with him on Instagram at andrew.clawson, on Twitter/X at @clawsonbooks, on Facebook at facebook.com/AndrewClawsonnovels and you can always send him an email at andrew@andrewclawson.com.